THE MARSHAL'S PROTECTION

BROTHERHOOD PROTECTORS WORLD

KENDRA MEI CHAILYN

Twisted Page Press LLC

BROTHERHOOD PROTECTORS

ORIGINAL SERIES BY ELLE JAMES

TAREK

Some days, it didn't pay to get out of bed.

Though going into my line of work had always been dangerous, I never woke up any day thinking *well, time to get shot at.*

But twice this week, I narrowly escaped with my life. The latest mishap left me in pain and just over the bullshit.

After a briefing with our captain, I lumbered out of the room holding my breath. Breathing was like getting punched in the ribs—repeatedly. I didn't want my guys worrying. I didn't want to hear the same old song and dance anymore—

You have money, why are you even working?

If I had your money, I'd be in Tahiti right now.

They didn't understand.

All my life, I'd have to work for everything. Life was hard but I had my family. Then we lost everything, and I almost died. My father and mother, unbeknownst to

1

each other, bought two different lottery tickets—big winners.

Still, my brothers and I worked hard in school, graduating at the tops of our classes. Jessy was still going through university, but Malik was now a brand-new doctor. I had served my country and came home to be pulled into the US Marshals.

In my family, we had never been the kind to sit around doing nothing.

I gripped my side and fell onto the seat in front of my locker and grunted. Moving made the spot where the bullet was stopped by my vest hurt like a motherfucker.

Holding my breath, I reached across my body and peeled off my Kevlar vest and dropped it on the bench beside me.

Getting undressed was like being punched in the stomach repeatedly. I had to grit my teeth through the pain. When I looked down at my left side, the spot where I was hit was red, turning purple. The vest had done its job and I was still standing—but each time I inhaled too deeply, I wondered how lucky I really had been.

I dragged a palm over it and winced.

It angered me.

Instead of merely going to prison, the perp had to make a pitstop at the hospital. He tried taking me out, but I was a faster draw. I then tackled his ass to the ground and shoved my knee into the wound. Hearing him scream, gave me great satisfaction. I wanted every time he thought of it, it hurt like hell.

Though I was pissed off, I didn't want him dead. The only reason he was still breathing was because I had positioned myself between my team and him.

"You can't ever do that again," Grim said. "We could have shot you."

I turned to look at him. A monster of a man wrapped around the heart of a teddy bear and the loyalty of saint. "But you didn't."

"Not the point, Cobra." He yanked open his locker. "The others are pissed, but I told them I'd bring it up."

"I understand." I winced and reached for a new shirt.

"What were you thinking? Cobra, you may not think you are worth anything, but we love you."

"I was thinking we've had enough deaths." I grunted.

Grim shoved my hands away and helped me with closing my shirt then went back to what he had been doing.

"I was thinking a little girl is dead." I managed. "And that bastard needed to hear the pain he's caused and get his ass kicked for what he's done. They are angry, Grim. And they need this. I wasn't about to allow him to be selfish and die leaving these people are stuck with that darkness. They need a place to put it and he's going to learn, there are worse things than death."

He sat beside me but said nothing.

"I'm sorry I scared you, brother."

"Just don't do it again." Grim turned his back to me. "The others are angry, but they can never understand how terrified I was seeing you fall like that."

"I'm—"

"You're all the family I got. Don't ever forget that."

I nodded. "You want to come through for dinner with me and the family tonight? I was supposed to be cooking but mom is covering for me."

"I'd love to, but I'm afraid I'll have to take a pass. Maybe next time?"

I chuckled. "You have other plans? Since when?"

"You're an ass." Grim rose and walked back to his locker to pull out a shirt. He shrugged into it. "I'm not sure what I was thinking—but I promised Morgan I'd go with her to this concert she's been raving about for the last six weeks. I don't even know what a Veeker is."

"That's the name of the band?"

He nodded.

"Well, good luck with that. Let me know how that goes." I slipped my feet into my shoes and gathered my things. "I'm going to head home before the family put out an APB on me. You have fun tonight."

"Thanks."

We hugged and I left the station via the backway. More lectures were coming, and I didn't feel ready to handle them.

The weather was torture. The heat rose upward like a fog. Sure, with the sun going down, the heat was a little more tolerable, but barely. The shirt I wore was thin, but it was still bothersome against my skin. I wanted to remove my shirt, but it hid the gun against my hip.

Another thing I signed up for when I became a cop after leaving the SEALS.

By the time I arrived home, my driveway was full. My father's Cadillac was parked to the right and my brother Malik's Porsche sat on the left. I pulled my Nissan GTR to the lawn now brown from the lack of water. Rain hadn't fallen in weeks and it would be a waste of water to water the lawn—there was no saving it. I probably should put in some cobblestone to save myself the issue when winter wore off and summer returned.

I killed the engine and pulled myself from the front seat. Every part of my body hurt.

It took some heavy brainpower to enter the house. The moment I made my presence known, the others cheered, welcoming me home. I tried not showing any pain. They'd just have questions and I didn't want to bring my job home to them.

"I love you guys, but I need a moment," I told them.

"You okay?" My father asked.

"Oh yeah." I kissed the side of my mother's head. "My vest was put to the test today that's all."

They'd find out sooner or later—it was better I told them straight out.

My mother gasped.

"Mom, don't freak out. I'm fine. I just need to put away my gun and shield."

Malik eyed me suspiciously and Jesse squinted in my direction. Somehow, I managed to smile at them and headed out of the room.

"He works too hard," my father said.

"Yeah." Jesse agreed. "But have you ever talked to him about taking time off? Head meet brick wall."

Malik laughed. "He'll be okay."

But I wasn't so sure. Lately, my body had been

taking a beating. It was barely a week ago when I was forced to jump from the second story of a building because a bomb was inside. I was banged up, but luckily not too bad.

Now this.

No, I couldn't tell them this punk took a shot at me and walked away from that brain-fart.

Climbing the stairs reminded me just how old I'd become. The fact I hadn't taken vacation time since I was assigned to the Marshals didn't help my case either. I'd lost track of how many times my captain threatened to force me to take time off. But what would I do with that time? I hate flying of late, so I wouldn't be leaving the country.

I'd rather work.

But I wasn't superhuman.

My bedroom had been cleaned—I was pretty sure that was my mother's doing. The clothes I'd left on my bed were gone as well as the shoes I'd discarded in front of my dresser. My bed was made with clean sheets and the unfolded laundry I had sitting on the chest at the foot of my bed was now folded and sitting atop the chest.

I smiled and slipped the picture frame out of the way. After entering my code, I pulled the safe open. My badge was the first to go in. When I pulled my gun from the holster, out of habit, I ejected the cartridge, cleared the chamber, and set them beside my shield.

"You look like you could use a beer." Malik's voice was soft.

I groaned and closed the safe it. Once I had the

picture back in place, I turned to see he was handing me a beer. "Thanks brother." I lifted the bottle in a silent toast then took a healthy swallow. We sat on the edge of my bed as laughter floated into the bedroom from the others downstairs. It was my turn to host a dinner for the family at my ranch. Since I was called out on a bust, mom decided to cook—at my place.

"Hard one?"

I nodded. "Child killer. Those are the hardest."

Malik rubbed my back. "I don't know how you do it," he said. "That would have ripped my heart out and you're still standing."

I said nothing. Instead, I drank more from the bottle, set it on the bedside table and slumped to my back.

"Want me to clear everyone out?" Malik asked. "We can do this another night. You're exhausted and I'm sure you could use some peace and quiet."

"No." I exhaled loudly. "After what I've seen today? I need this. My family brings me peace—is that weird?"

Malik smiled and rubbed my back. "No. There's nothing weird or wrong about wanting your family around you right now. They say love heals, right?"

"I've heard that too."

Malik chuckled. "So, what's the verdict?"

"Let me get a shower to wash off some of the muck, then I'll come down."

"Let me see," Malik said.

I didn't have to ask what he meant. Instead, I lifted the hem of my shirt so he could see the spot. He pressed it firmly with two fingers and I groaned in pain.

"Well." Malik traced the edges with a finger. "You

didn't break anything. It's going to be this colour for a bit. Try not to exert yourself too much."

"Thanks, Doc."

"Have you given any thoughts to taking some time off?" Malik asked. "You've been going at this for a while now. Your body will splinter."

"I know. And I have thought about it."

Malik nodded, patted my shoulder and left me alone to my demons. Still on my back, I removed the Rolex my mother had given me when I graduated from the academy, the necklace Jesse presented me with for my last birthday and a ring Malik bought me on one of this trips to Greece because he thought it was my style. I set them all on the bed and peeled myself off to shower.

The water did help. It cooled my body and gave me a little kick to make it through family dinner.

Hopefully, I wouldn't fall asleep in my plate.

When I made an appearance, everyone swarmed around to hug me, and my father handed me another beer.

"The table is set," William Jonas said. "We can all sit."

I nodded to my father and we headed to the dinner table, my mother, wrapping an arm around my hips.

My parents, William and Paula, positioned themselves at the heads of the table as usual. My brother Malik sat to one side of the table with an empty chair beside him. Jesse sat at my side and I smiled at the spread.

My mother hadn't spared no expense.

The table was heavily laden with all our favorites—

beef stew, Jamaican rice and peas, curried goat, a garden salad, and friend plantains.

We ate, chatted, joked. There were questions about my work and my lack of taking vacation.

To others looking in, they would believe I was a visitor—a person who didn't belong. Their beautiful dark skin was a stark contrast to my very white flesh. But I learned a long time ago, blood didn't make family —love did.

And as I looked around the table, listened to the laughter, see the mirth on each and every face, I felt love. I knew the room brimmed with love and I couldn't be happier for the family I had been blessed with.

Most orphans didn't have it this good.

Eventually, it was time for my brothers to go. Malik ran out to his car for some aspirins.

"Take one before bed." He shoved the bottle into my pocket when I walked him to the door. "I didn't want mom to see me giving you these. She'd just spend the night worrying and that's not good for dad's sanity or my sleep."

"Are you sure I need these?"

"Of course, I'm sure." Malik frowned. "Or would you prefer to stay awake tonight? I guarantee every time you fall asleep and roll over on that bruise…"

I sighed and hugged him just as Jesse joined us.

Jesse stepped in for a squeeze too and I moaned as his body hit my injury.

"Sorry." Jesse told me, framing one side of my face with a palm. "You know I worry…"

"I know."

"I'm not going to nag." Jesse pressed his lips into a thin line, sighed then nodded. "You're still standing. You're here. So, all I'm going to say is, I love you."

"I love you too, Jess."

Malik and Jesse left in the same car as usual. Malik would drop Jesse off at his apartment close to the university, then head home. My parents lingered while longer worrying about me. My mother fussed the most. She hugged me repeatedly and I, somehow, managed not to grunt at the hurt her super tight hugs caused.

Eventually, my father managed to talk her out the door.

"Call your friend," my mother said after kissing my cheek for what had to be the millionth time. "Take him up on the offer for you to visit. Didn't you say he was here, in Billings?"

I nodded.

It scared me the things she remembered.

"I know it's not leaving the country, but I'm sure this friend of yours would make sure you rested."

I smiled. "I'll think about it."

"Don't think about it," my mother said. "Do it."

"Paula, leave the boy alone." My father laughed before stepping in for a hug. "Listen to your mother."

I chuckled. "Okay, dad. You two be safe heading home." I told him as I walked them to their car. My father loved his truck but when he took mom out with him, he used the Cadillac. Mom's knees couldn't take the climb into the truck anymore.

When the headlights flooded my driveway, I stepped back to the porch and watched until long after the taillights disappeared in the distance. I then hauled my tired self back inside, locked the door and set the alarms. Though all I wanted to do was fall into bed, I stacked the dirty dishes into the dishwasher, started it then headed up the stairs, turning off lights as I went.

Usually, I would wake up in the wee hours of the morning to use the bathroom or just to stare at the ceiling. This time, I slept like the dead until around eleven. The sleep did nothing to help and I knew my mother had been right. Before I climbed out of bed, I grabbed my cell, scrolled through my contacts until I got to Alex Davila.

"Cobra!" Alex "Taz" Davila greeted me. "How the hell are ya?"

"Exhausted."

"I keep telling you. Come through!" Taz reminded him. "I'm still in Billings for another few days. Besides, I need the ride back."

I laughed.

"Hannah and I would be happy to have you, man." Taz added. "Seriously."

"That's why I'm calling. I've decided to take you up on your offer."

"Score. When were you thinking?"

"Why don't I wait until you're ready to head back and go with you?"

"I'm sure it won't be an issue." Taz assured me. "Like I said, I need the ride."

"Why don't you come here for the next few days?" I asked him. "I don't suppose the hotel is very comfortable."

"And I told you, I don't want to impose."

"Taz, bruh. Besides, I have enough food in my fridge right now to feed a small village."

"How?"

"My mother struck again."

Taz laughed.

I smiled. I hadn't seen Taz in person in over a year and a half. We were close at one point—but then he took a job with the Protectors after he came home and then became busy. We spoke on the phone and video chat and our friendship had survived the distance and adult life. We chatted a little longer, until Taz was being called by someone in the background.

After our goodbyes, I immediately climbed out of bed and packed a bag.

ELLIE

IT WAS BARELY ten in the morning, and already the temperature was nauseating. It bore down on Eagle Rock, unforgiving and scorching. For the millionth time as I made my way back toward the house with Lilah on her leash, I wondered why I'd gotten a puppy. She needed to be walked—regularly, the heat of summers in Montana wasn't conducive to that kind of commitment.

My father honked and waved as his Mercedes Benz sped along the driveway leading to the main road from our ranch. I waved the little bag of doggie doo at him. I didn't mean to, but my other hand was full.

When I faced my path again, I wanted to cry.

The ranch seemed so far away. I figured the heat caused the exhaustion in me but there really wasn't anything I could do. Breathing was a chore but, I forced one foot ahead of the other with Lilah panting beside me.

I finally managed to step into the cool interior and quickly locked the door behind me. There wasn't any sight of my mom and I didn't bother looking. She always went back to bed after having a cup of coffee in the mornings. I, personally, didn't see the point. They merely stood in the kitchen, the only sound being my father slurping from his mug. Mom would climb back into bed, irritated, after muttering that my father was raised in a barn.

Inside, I filled Lilah's water bowl and watched as she drank greedily. The puppy ran to the door, barked, chased her tail then hurried back to the water. I shook my head and grabbed a bottle of water. I didn't move until the entire bottle was empty. When I turned for the stairs, Lilah ran after me, so I picked her up.

I set the puppy on my bed but instead of settling down, Lilah looked toward the window and barked. She was always doing that, mostly because of the squirrels or sounds. Another thing I had to teach her not to do for she would wake the entire house. I gave her my sternest look. "Sit." I told her. "Sit."

Lilah yawned as though I was boring her, then turned and stuck her head under one of the pillows with her ass in the air. I frowned and wandered into the bathroom for a shower. Training Lilah was impossible. I should have known better than to get a husky.

Everyone warned me they were stubborn and impossible to train.

Instead of focusing on the puppy, I turned my attention to my plans for the day. I had a late lunch with Jennifer, a little shopping with Susan then will have to tolerate dinner with my parents.

I rolled my eyes.

After my shower, I wrapped my body in a towel and sat at my dresser. I lifted my eyes to my reflection and could barely recognize the face looking back at me. My pale blue yes seemed different somehow—I just couldn't quite put my finger on it.

A line of zits dotted the left side of my chin and I could see the beginning of one between my eyes. At my age, should I still be getting zits?

I sighed.

This is some bullshit.

I probably needed to go back on my sugar-free diet.

It took some time with all the brushes and different stages. It took a little bit longer to cover up the zits and red spots than I would have liked. Perfection took time and I wasn't about to rush it.

Once I was satisfied, I sprayed on a sealer to keep the make-up from sweating off, then pealed off the towel to get dressed.

I slipped into a designer mini dress with a plunging back. The heat was intolerable so the less fabric I had to put on my body, the better. I took some time to pull my hair up into a sensible ponytail, plugged in pearl stud earrings then squirted some perfume to my neck. I skipped a necklace because it wouldn't go right with the dress then paused to see if I was missing something.

Deodorant was the last thing to go on and soon, I was ready. I took some time to put on a pair of bright, red pumps. As I looked at myself in the mirror, I couldn't help feeling absolutely beautiful. "Well, pup…" I looked on the bed, but she wasn't there. I found Lilah snoozing on the floor beside the new bed I'd bought her. I didn't understand that dog. She had a bed, but the floor seemed to be more comfortable.

When I descended the stairs, it was a while later and I was beginning to feel as if I should take a nap. Still, shopping called. It stunned me to find my mom sitting in the living room with two uniformed police officers. I couldn't remember a time when there were cops in the house. Soldiers, mostly men and women of power, but never any police officers. This was certainly new.

I arched a brow. "What's going on?" I asked. "Why are the police here?"

Mom sniffled and wiped her nose with a crumbled handkerchief. "Um—it's your father. He's missing. He didn't make it to his meeting with the Department of Defence."

"Seriously?" I asked. "You don't seriously believe that, do you?"

"Ellie." My mom warned around another sniffle. "Not now."

"What do you mean?" One of the cops asked.

I frowned. "Dad's not missing. He was here this morning." I stopped short at saying he was probably with one of his many whores. I didn't stick around to hear much of anything else. I hurried out to my Porsche and tossed myself behind the wheel. As I zoomed along the long driveway, I wondered why mom was even crying over dad. The man was unfaithful and didn't even try hiding his infidelities.

This wouldn't be the first time he went radio silent for an extended period of time. But he'd only been gone a couple of hours. I'm not sure why mom was freaking out.

My father had the habit of going off on binges—days would pass, and we wouldn't be able to find him. Then he'd show up smelling like cheap perfume and with his collar caked in lipstick.

I wasn't worried. He will pop up again sooner or later, hung over and dazed. The last time he went on one of his little orgy-fests, he needed penicillin to clear up a little itch he had. I found out when he pulled something from his pocket and the prescription fell out.

Every time I thought of that whole scenario, I wanted to hurl.

Still, mom stayed with him. I wasn't sure if it was the money or weakness. Afterall, she'd been with him for so many years, no judge would let her walk out of the marriage with nothing. Then again, the legal system was messed up—to say the least.

At the restaurant, I handed the sports car over to the valet and hurried inside. The hostess smiled at me then led me over to the table Jennifer and I always used. We hugged and I plopped down in my chair.

"What's up with you?" Jennifer quired a carefully sculpted eyebrow.

"You'd never guess."

Jennifer arched a brow. "Guess? Oh boy. Something to do with Lilah? I told you not to get that dog because she would be a pain in the butt."

"That dog is hopeless." I shook my head. "I know that now. I can't even teach her to sit. It's a disaster there but one I can handle. No, it's nothing to do with Lilah. It's my dad."

"Well? Tell me."

I sighed. "He's missing."

"Again?" She asked.

"I know, right?" I exhaled loudly. "My mom seems to think this time it warrants calling the police. So, right now she's sitting in the living-room, flanked by two of Montana's finest, playing the dutiful wife."

"Maybe he really is missing this time." Jennifer was thoughtful. "She's never called the police before, right?"

"Doubt it." I cleared my throat and dropped my cell into my purse. "He keeps sticking his dick into the dark places and mom is sitting at home with cops, sobbing. I mean, the fuck?"

"Money makes us do strange things, I guess." Jennifer explained. "Think about it. What would happen if you lost all yours? You have to keep in mind, your mother hasn't worked in years. Your father has been the primary source of income and the person who keeps her to the lifestyle she's become accustomed. She probably couldn't find a job out there in this atmosphere if she tried."

I frowned. Jennifer's words hit a little close to home. The fact I was almost thirty and never had an actual job was a little unnerving. My money couldn't last forever —even though there was a lot of it.

Maybe Jennifer had a point—maybe I should figure out a back-up plan.

I didn't have time to say anything else as the waitress hurried over to speak with us. When we were finally alone again the subject drifted from my father to other things. It wasn't hard to switch the focus of her talk. Soon we were having a deep conversation about the latest episode of a reality show.

We finished lunch a little after three in the afternoon and I donned my designer shades and headed to my car. I was barely out of the parking lot when my phone rang. When I saw my mother's name, I rolled my eyes and declined the call. She wasn't going to ruin my day because she didn't have a brain in her head.

Shopping with Susan was precisely what the doctor ordered—new shoes, a few new dresses and a laptop later, I headed for home. I'd be a little late for dinner but that only meant I would miss a bit of the forced conversation and awkward silences. For years, my mother had been forcing us to eat together at least one night per night. I didn't see the point—the two of them together in the same room threatened to drive me insane with the lack of love I felt between them.

I couldn't ever remember them being in love.

But when I arrived home, the house was dark except for the kitchen. I ignored it and headed up the stairs for a quick shower. By the time I returned, the light was out and there was no dinner.

"Randy?" I called for our chef. "Beatrice?"

"I fired them." My mother's voice was cold from behind me.

I shifted to face her. "You fired them? Who is going to make my food and clean up around here?"

"You have two hands!" Mom snapped. "Cook your own god-damn food or starve!" She turned to leave then paused. "By the way, they found your father's car. There was blood in it. But hope your shopping was fun."

She left me stunned into silence. Mom had given me a bunch of information I didn't need or care about. I still didn't understand why the servants were gone and I had to make my own food.

It shouldn't be that hard.

I opened the fridge and looked in. Everything seemed so foreign, so strange. I poked a raw chicken leg and recoiled as my body heaved.

"Nope." I closed the fridge and ordered a pizza.

I JERKED upright in bed as a loud bang caught my attention. Lilah looked up, yawned and rolled over. Before I knew what was happening, she fell asleep on her back with her legs wide open. I frowned and was about to flop back to my pillows when the sound echoed through the house once more. I climbed from my bed, grabbed my robe and hurried out of my room while pushing my arms into it. I rushed down the stairs to find my mother standing in the semi-dark, staring at the door.

"For god's sakes!" I tried rushing by her.

Mom grabbed my arm. "Don't get that." She growled in a whisper.

Whoever was out there kept right on slamming their fist into the door a bit longer, then an ignition started. The sound wandered father away from the house until there was nothing but silence.

Mom released my arm and turned for the steps.

"Mom, what's going on? Who was that?"

"Suddenly you care—what a surprise."

"What's that supposed to mean?" I asked.

"Whatever the hell you want it to mean." Mom replied. She paused her climb to look at me. "Go back to your designer bullshit. FYI, spend your money wisely. There isn't any more."

"Wait—what?"

"I'm going to bed." She tossed over her shoulder.

"Who was at the door?"

"Demons your father brought back from Colombia." She disappeared down the hall at the top of the stairs and I crumbled to the steps.

What was going on?

Demons from Colombia?

When did my father go to Colombia? And even if he did have a job there, he's a government contractor. He built things for them, not fight wars. How did he bring back demons?

I managed to pull myself together enough to follow my mother. She was in the master bedroom furiously rummaging through dad's walk-in safe. As I entered, I realized she was muttering under her breath, flipping things out over her shoulders.

"Mom?"

"If you're not here to help, go away."

"What are you looking for?"

"A clue as to what your father has done—where the money went." She picked up a leather-bound book and flipped it open. The pages were blanked. "Shit!" She chucked it out of the safe over her left shoulder. "Those men will come back. They're dangerous."

"Maybe we should call the cops."

Mom growled. "For what? What are they going to do? Ugh! There's nothing here."

She rushed from the safe and started digging through dad's bedside table. "I checked the accounts. We're broke. There's no money. The house isn't ours anymore because your father took out a mortgage on it and said nothing. We're behind two payments and he's been hiding the reminder notices."

"We're losing the house?" My voice trembled.

Mom stopped to look at me. "Eventually."

"This is bullshit."

"Tell me about it." Mom tossed her hands up. "Nothing! He left us nothing but trouble. You need to find somewhere to go. I'll have to—I have nothing." She crumbled to the floor, her body rocking with sobs.

"That's not true. You…"

"I'd like to be alone, please." Mom's voice cracked.

COBRA

BEFORE LEAVING BILLINGS, I stopped at my parents' place. Once they hugged me, I made one other stop to grab Taz who was at one of the local police station to meet with a friend. The plan was for me to drive with him into Eagle Rocks and to my week of relaxing and doing nothing.

After grabbing coffee for the ride, I turned the sports car toward Eagle Rocks.

The Crazy Mountains rose like a force in front of my Nissan GTR. I never tire of the view. I exhaled loudly. "Would you look at that." I mused.

"See?" Taz asked. "You're already relaxing."

"Smart-ass." I muttered.

Taz only laughed. "I told my girl you're staying two weeks. We're working most days. Can you entertain yourself while we're out?"

"I'm sure I can find some trouble to get into."

"I don't doubt that. How you been since leaving the SEALs?"

I shrugged. "I'm still standing. Just a little tired, that's all."

"Well, you'll be okay." Taz told me as I turned into the driveway the GPS instructed me.

I leaned forward to look at the ranch and whistled long and loud. "You've done good, son."

Taz laughed.

We climbed out and Taz led me into the house. He didn't wait to give me the tour starting out with the room I'd be using at the back of the house overlooking the mountains. It was set up so I could lay in bed and stare at peaks or they would be the first thing I saw when I opened my eyes in the mornings.

I could live with that.

After the tour, Taz received a call from the Protectors and had to run out. I wasn't sure what to do with myself. I stretched out on my bed, flipping through the channels on the television. Nothing caught my attention and after a few minutes of desperately trying to be interested in something on the screen, I gave up and flipped it off. I dropped the remote on the bed and pulled out my cellphone to call Malik.

"You're there?" Malik asked before he even said hello. "How's Taz's place?"

"Perfect. I'm lying on my bed right now, staring at the Crazies."

"Sounds peaceful."

"It is." I sighed. "But I'm bored out of my mind."

"Enjoy the down time." Malik advised me. "We'll be able to sleep well tonight knowing you're not busting through some asshole's door."

I chuckled. "Well, I just wanted to check in. I love you guys."

"We love you too. Call if you need anything."

I promised I would, hung up and dumped the phone into my pocket. After a while, the silence was maddening. I pushed from the bed and wandered downstairs and into the kitchen. The fridge was stock full. Someone had taken out beef and I settled for making beef stew with basmati rice and seasonal vegetables. I'd just turned off the stove when someone cleared their throat behind me.

I spun around.

"You must be Tarek Jonas."

She was pretty, curves in all the right places with sparkling eyes. Taz was a very lucky man.

"You must be Miss Hannah." I wiped my hands into a towel and extended one to her.

"Just Hannah is fine." She shook my hand and released it. "Something smells really good."

I grinned. "Jamaican beef stew."

"How'd you learn to make it?" Hannah asked while peering into the pot. "Is it ready?"

"It's ready." I replied. "And my mother taught me how to make it. Let me get you a plate."

"If that tastes as good as it smells." She climbed into one of the highchairs at the island. "I'm keeping you."

I laughed. After dishing her a plate, I set it in front of her and waited for a verdict. She lifted some food to her lips and moaned. I laughed and nodded. "I have my answer."

Once she was settled into eating, I poured her a glass

of lemonade and set in beside her plate. She waved her fork at me in thanks and I chuckled.

"You didn't have to do this." She told me. "But I ain't mad you did."

"I know. I was feeling a little bored." I told her. "Besides, I'm barging into your lives for two weeks. I might as well make myself useful."

"You're not barging, believe me. You're a friend of Taz. He thinks you're good people. You are more than welcome here."

"Thank you."

"So, mom taught you to cook?" Hannah asked. "I didn't think mothers do that anymore."

I nodded. "Yeah. She didn't want us to be burdens to our wives. She has three boys, no daughters. It's either a blessing or a curse. She insisted on teaching us how to take care of ourselves and how to change a tire. My dad taught us a lot of things but there are certain things only a mom can teach her kids."

Hannah laughed. "Your mom sounds like a strong woman."

"She is."

Hannah tilted her head. "I have to ask—your mom is Jamaican?"

I smiled. "Yes. I was adopted by black parents."

"Oh! That is cool."

"I have to agree." I smiled proudly. "They are the best parents a little orphan boy could ever have."

"Aww, I can hear the love in your voice."

I winked at her and she smiled.

"Where's Taz, anyway? I thought you two would head out for beers or something."

"He got a call from Montana." I explained to her. "He tried getting a hold of you but…"

"Damn it." Hannah sighed and dug for her cell. She frowned when she activated the screen. "I missed three calls from him. Today was a bit weird at the office. Are you going to eat?"

Honestly, I wasn't going to until Taz returned, but I gave in and joined her. In the end, she shooed me from the kitchen and cleaned up herself. I took the moment to shower.

THE FIRST THING my eyes caught were the mountains. I inhaled deeply, held the breath then exhaled slowly. I couldn't remember a time I'd been so at peace.

I remained on my back, soaking in the silence. It wasn't easy to be completely relaxed, but I wanted the view outside the window to imprint itself on my brain. Eventually, I peeled myself from the bed, showered and dressed. After a few quick texts to my brothers and parents, I descended the stairs in search of coffee.

Instead, I found Taz, Swede and Kujo.

"I wasn't going to leave without—what's wrong?" The look on their faces left me with an unsteady feeling in the pit of my stomach.

"You should probably sit down for this." Swede told me.

I wasn't going to but when he motioned toward the

seat with his head, I knew something was up. Reluctantly, I sat but didn't take my eyes off Taz.

Kujo slid a picture across the island toward me. The action forced me to look down.

I should have stayed in bed.

I pushed the photograph back to Kujo and stood. "Whatever she wants, the answer is no. I'm not interested."

"Cobra…" Taz pleaded. "Come on. This isn't a joke."

"Did you hear a punchline?"

"She's in trouble." Swede pushed. "You're a cop. Serve and protect, remember?"

"If she's in trouble, have her call 9-1-1 like a regular person. I don't want to have anything to do with her. Besides, I'm on vacation."

"What's the story here?" Taz asked.

"That's none of your business." I snapped. "If she wants protection, that's your job. I'm sure her father can pay you. Anything else, Eagle Rocks has a police station."

Swede grabbed my arm as I walked by him. "Cobra, we all took an oath. She's in trouble, brother, serious trouble. I know this isn't your jurisdiction, but you have history with her and might be the best person for this job."

I bowed my head, anger, absolute rage tearing through me. The force of it made my vision blur and I wanted to scream.

"Do this as a favor for us." Swede pushed.

"What's wrong?" I asked while facing them.

"Good man." Taz patted my shoulder.

"How long have you known her?" Swede asked.

"Since we were kids." My voice cracked. "My father used to work for hers."

"Her father has been a government contractor for years." Swede continued. "He owns Sargent Contractors. His last assignment was in Colombia. Out of all of us, you know that geography."

"We don't know exactly what happened while he was working there, but now he has people after him." Kujo picked up the story.

"He's missing." Taz reported. "Last night armed men broke into the place—shot Laura in the back. She was running away, and the shot her in the back."

"Fucking cowards." Kujo muttered. "Who shoots a woman in the back?"

"Ellie?" I asked. There was no reason to ask about Laura. If they clocked her in the back, they didn't go there to leave anyone alive.

"She's fine." Swede replied. "They got the mother and the puppy."

"For fuck's sakes." I grunted. "They had to kill the dog too? I mean, what's he going to say?"

No one replied.

I rubbed my eyes wondering why I hadn't just stayed in bed. "Give me the information you have. I'll go take a look at the house then speak with Ellie."

Taz tossed me a set of keys. "We figured you probably shouldn't drive your own vehicle around right now. So, to kinda make up for stepping into your vacation, we've gotten you a toy."

"You were sure I'd say yes, weren't you?" I mused.

"More like hoping. We didn't know you and Ellie had some dangerous history." Kujo replied. "You're a good man, Cobra."

"Let me get changed." I eyed him.

"Need directions?" Swede asked.

"Did they move in the last few years?" I wanted to know.

"Nope." Taz told me. "Same place as always."

"Then, I'm good." I gathered the file Swede handed me and without another word, I left the group. By the time I went through all the information given to me, and headed back down to the others, Swede and Kujo were gone. Taz was having leftover stew.

"This is delicious." Taz mused. "I think Hannah is in love."

I smirked. "Sorry, brother."

Taz chewed. "For real though, watch your back. You carrying?"

I eased a side of my coat out of the way to show him the gun and badge strapped to my hip. I grabbed his coffee and took a healthy sip. "I'll see you."

When I exited the house, I was greeted by a black Dodge Charger. It sat in the driveway, one of the sexiest cars I'd ever seen.

"Try keeping it in one piece?" Taz asked. "Reaper's fiancée gave it to him as an engagement present and he will strangle you if you scratch it."

"Reaper?"

"Yeah." Taz sipped from his mug. "One of our new guys."

I tossed myself into the driver's seat and slammed

the door. With a twist of my wrist, the car roared, and it was as sexy as I imagined it would be. I honked at Taz and made a quick turn, then sped along the dirt road leading me to the main road. My mind switched to what I read in the scant file. Most of it I already knew. The Sargents had money and wielded it like a kid who'd found his father's loaded gun.

Their behaviour only grew worse over the years. The moment Ellie had her license, she became a certified nuisance. From driving through the neighbours' fields, to tearing through town at breakneck speed. Who was going to stop her? The law seemed to have been afraid of anything to do with them.

All those years and she was still a spoiled little bitch with no regard for anyone around her. I frowned, pulled to a stop in front of the house. After turning off the engine, I sat back to look the place over. As a kid, this place gave me the creeps—nothing had changed.

"What a waste." I muttered.

It took everything in me to find a pair of gloves in my pocket, climb from the vehicle and lumbered up the stairs. For a moment, I stared at the door as if it was the cause of all my horrors in life.

No matter how long I stood there, I knew what had to be done. I had come this far and there was no turning back. The urge to strangle Taz and every single one of the Protectors filled my brain as I ducked under the police tape. Out of habit, I pushed at the door with the tow of my shoes. To my surprise, it opened easily. Being a crime scene, the door should have been locked. I frowned and pulled my gun.

I had to step over blood drops on the floor in the foyer then proceeded to clear each room one by one. When I found no one, I returned to the front door, closed it by pushing it closed with the tow of my shoe, then turned my attention to the blood drops.

The wall was sprayed with red dots and I meant one thing—high velocity blood splatter. Someone had been shot in the hall—Laura. I allowed my eyes to trail down the wall until I was hunched down. The blood belonging to Laura was easy enough to spot. The rest of the droplets showed me someone was bleeding and running toward the front door.

"Someone else was bleeding." I muttered.

The rest of the house was annoyingly familiar. I rummaged through without touching much even with the gloves on. The bedrooms were different—the master bedroom looked as though someone had gone through it looking for something. Ellie's bedroom was empty except for the large blood stain in the middle of the bed. I assumed that was where they'd found the puppy.

When I finally made it into Jeffrey's office, I wasn't at all surprised by what I found. It didn't fair much better than the rest of the place. I stepped over the carnage and sat in the leather chair behind the desk. "If I was Jeffrey, where would I hide my most precious secrets?"

It wouldn't be a safe behind a picture frame. Jeffrey worked with some of the worlds best special forces teams and often times CIA—he would learn from them.

Where he hid things would have to be somewhere he knew no one would think of looking.

I walked over to the bookcase and began dragging my finger along the frame of it.

My next try was under the office desk. To my surprise, my hand hit something.

Curious, I slipped to my back and used my phone's flashlight to see what I was touching. "Very clever, Jeff. Just not smart enough."

I pulled the black book off, peeled the tape away and pushed to my feet.

I couldn't make heads or tails of the numbers and abbreviations. I shoved it into the inside pocket of my coat and exited the house.

It didn't take long for me to reach the Protector's headquarters. When I arrived, I expected more people to be there, but I only Swede sat in the kitchen tapping away at his laptop. I handed him the book but said nothing until after I'd poured myself the first mug of coffee of the day.

While Swede skimmed through the book, a redhead walked in and immediately went for the coffee. She was later introduced as Molly who was with Kujo. She bumped fist with Swede, kissed Kujo then all but bolted out the door after checking a message on her phone. I sat to talk to Swede about what I'd found.

"Are you sure the blood drops aren't from the dog?" Swede asked.

"No. The dog was killed in Ellie's room." I told him. "These blood drops are from someone who was hurt in

33

the house and was running out the door. They were looking for something."

"So, they killed Laura then toss the place?" Swede asked. "Wouldn't it have been easier to just ask her? I mean, she'd be scared shitless and would have given them anything they wanted."

"Unless she didn't know what they were asking about" I told him. "That man went through a lot to hide that book. I 'm thinking that's what they're looking for."

"Maybe—I just need to figure what that is." Swede flipped the page. "This wouldn't have helped them. There's no names, addresses, code. Just a bunch of dates and numbers. But for what?"

"You're the brains of the operation." I poured myself a second cup of coffee. After a few healthy sips, I turned to Swede. "Where's Ellie?"

"I'll take you."

I followed Swede up the stairs and to the back of the house where Swede knocks on a closed door and stepped in before anyone answered. "Viper, Cobra is here."

ELLIE

Laura Sargent was dead.

It began in a split second, chased by chaos and ended in silence.

The police were no help at all.

My mother and Lilah had been brutally murdered and all they could tell me was that they were investigating. I tried getting a little support from my friends, my father's friends, but suddenly, no one was picking up their phones. I thought Jennifer and Susan would have my back, that they'd be the first people to be there, holding my hands and crying with me.

I had been wrong and it damn near killed me.

In my time of need, I had to count on strangers I found through a message board.

The sad thing about it, when I called on them, there was no jeering. They'd sent an army to my aid even though they were fully booked. The very sexy one they called Kujo suggested bringing in a friend, someone they called, King Cobra, and I wasn't about to look a sexy gift horse in the mouth.

But even if I wanted to hit on him, it soon become evident, Kujo was off the market.

I sighed.

When it came time for me to meet their King, I was more than ready. The sooner I could get to the bottom of what was happening, figure out where my father was and why my mother and Lilah had to die, the better.

But my heart fell when Taz walked into the room with another man behind him. The moment Taz stepped out of the way, my mouth immediately grew dry.

Those eyes.

I would know them anywhere. They looked misplaced in the muscular body they now sat in. Years ago, this man had been a tall, lanky kid with wild eyes. The last time I'd seen them, he was being held back by his older brother, Malik.

Tarek Jonas had been so pissed off at me that day, I knew if Malik hadn't been there, he would have torn me limb from limb.

The day everything exploded, I thought I'd won. I smirked, egged him on. Repeatedly, Malik lost hold of Tarek and he made for me again. But Malik always managed to get Tarek under control until they were off the property. I'd waved at Tarek then headed inside to demand the chef make me a pizza from scratch.

After he was finished, I changed my mind and dumped the entire pizza in the garbage.

No, getting rid of The Jonas' was a situation to celebrated with a night out full of underaged drinking and maybe a make-out session with someone else's boyfriend.

The rage I had seen that day was still in Tarek's eyes. Only now, it simmered under control like a volcano they believed to be dormant.

Only now, I was mature enough to know I should be scared.

"I'm going to leave you guys to talk," Taz said, while heading for the door.

I grabbed Viper's arm as he turned to follow his friend.

"You'll be fine." Viper encouraged. "Cobra is good people."

But I wasn't so sure.

"Ellie?" Viper whispered my name.

"Hmmm?"

"You have to let me go."

I reluctantly released him, smiled but slowly died a little inside.

Tarek Jonas was sexy as fuck. I wasn't sure how else to put it. His green eyes still burned with the anger of a thousand suns. His body—oh gawd that body.

"Um…" I cleared my throat but didn't move. "You're King Cobra."

He said nothing.

Instead, he walked to the window, shoved his fingers into his pockets and stared out. The silence had to have been for a breath, but it was like an eternity. If I didn't know he was there, I would have probably missed him. He was unmoving, still, yet he cast such an overwhelming shadow over the space. It was hard being in the same space as this version of Tarek Jonas. Everything about him turned me on, even the anger in his eyes.

"I never would have expected it to be you. I'm pretty sure you don't want to be here. Um—I could ask them to find someone else or just wait for the police to—"

"Tell me about your father in the last year or so." His voice tight, like the unexpected the roll of thunder on a sunny day. I must have jumped a foot in the air. Thankfully, he was facing away from me and didn't see my reaction.

"Tarek I—"

"Your father."

I trembled, wanting nothing more than to fall to my knees in front of him, give him all the control. All my adult life, I'd never felt that way with any other man. The things flowing through my mind weren't Godly. They were naughty, taboo and probably illegal in most places. But deep down I know I was being an idiot. Not only were those feelings and thoughts inappropriate for the situation I found myself in, but Tarek was off limits, he'd always been off limits.

I didn't deserve to be thinking of Tarek in such a way. I was surprised he'd even agreed to take this job. After what I'd done to him and his family, I figured he'd just let me die. The thought alone broke me until I saw the badge on his hip. He was only doing so because it was his job.

I was gutted again.

"He spent most of that time away on some project." I managed. "He was rarely ever home."

"Where?"

"I don't know."

"Why?" Tarek pushed. "He didn't tell you or didn't you care to know? Because I can guarantee if my father is going to be away for any length of time I'm knowing where he's going, who he's going with and when he's coming back."

I hung my head. The truth was, I hadn't thought to ask. The money he was bringing in was a little more important. What the hell had I been thinking? When had I become just an ass?

"Figures." He still hadn't faced me. "What do you know about his work in Colombia?"

I had nothing.

"How about Iraq?"

Silence.

He turned on his heels and I withered under his glare.

"What *do* you know?" He stressed.

Nothing.

"How about where he was going the day he went missing?" Tarek asked.

"A meeting, I think."

"You think?"

Hell, I didn't think anything was wrong until I saw my mother hit the floor. I couldn't take his judgment. Knowing Tarek was disappointed in me again broke my heart into a million little pieces. Pushing from my place at the edge of the bed and wrapped my arms around myself.

"Okay." Tarek dragged his fingers through his hair. "What was he doing the last time you saw him?"

"Leaving. I was coming back from walking—from walking Lilah."

"The puppy?"

I nodded.

"How did he seem to you?"

I shrugged.

"Thank you." His sarcasm was right. "You've been no help at all. I thought I should let you know that."

"What do you want me to say?" I looked pointedly at him. "I'm a shit daughter, okay? Is that what you want from me?"

"Don't flatter yourself." Tarek chuckled bitterly. "I've never wanted anything from you—not one damn thing, not ever. Isn't that why you destroyed my life?"

He stormed from the room and I followed silently.

"She's useless." Tarek shouted at someone in the room. "Absolutely useless."

"Cobra." Taz's voice echoed softly. "Come on, man."

"I'm standing right here." I snapped.

"Then I'll say it to your face—"

"Cobra!" Taz called.

"I'm on vacation, Taz!" He stressed. "I'm on vacation and if I'm going to work, I need something to go on. She knows nothing. It's almost as if she lived on a different planet from her parents. What the hell am I supposed to do with that?"

Taz frowned. "Sometimes we have nothing." He was

staring down at his phone as his frown deepened. "You know how it goes. That's the nature of the beast."

"Yes. And usually I would work it—but I don't have the patient or the will to care."

"Cobra, do this as a favour to me." Taz pleaded.

Tarek grunted his annoyance. "That's not fair. You using our friendship as a weapon is so not fair." "Shit." Taz muttered as he stared down at this phone that had vibrated on the counter. "Can I leave you two alone? Montana has an assignment for me."

"We'll be fine." Tarek leveled his green gaze to me. "*Miss Sargent* and I need to talk."

I swallowed the lump in my throat and fell into one of the chairs someone had vacated but hadn't pushed back under the table.

"Oh, Jesus." Taz muttered, rising from his seat. "Please—I'm begging you. No bloodshed."

Tarek didn't speak, but I offered Taz a small smile. I didn't want Taz to leave me alone with Tarek. But I'd caused the storm between myself and Tarek. I couldn't escape the destruction of it anymore. Karma had finally gotten around to me.

From the look in Tarek's eyes, there would be hell to pay.

I stood—maybe if I made my escape now, the fallout wouldn't be as bad as I thought—no, as I *knew*—it would be.

"Sit." He told me.

My back went up at his command. Ever since I was a little girl, I hated being told what to do, especially in that tone of voice. I wanted to tell him off—to tell him to go to hell. But found myself slipping into my chair while clamping my thighs together. He pulled another, turned it around and sat with the back to his chest. The position drew the material of his jeans tightly against his muscular thighs—I chewed into my bottom lip.

What is wrong with me?

"I need you to think back. Has Laura or Jeff mentioned anything about Colombia? Anything at all, no matter how small could be helpful."

I stared at his handsome face, the rugged slopes of it. His jawlines were perfect, a flat nose and plump lips I would love to sit on. It took some doing, but I managed to shake the thoughts from my head and went through my memory to give him something—anything. As I was about to shake my head, something struck me. "Demons."

"What did you say?" Tarek asked.

"Someone came to the house and kept knocking at the door." I explained. "I was going to open it, but mom stopped me. Eventually, whoever it was, went away. When I asked mom what it was about, she said it was demons my father brought back from Colombia. It was weird, but I just thought she meant a woman. A year and a half before that, he was in Mexico and brought back some woman who didn't even know he was married."

"So, he brings women back often."

"I don't know." I shrugged. "Maybe, maybe not. I mean, the only reason I knew about the woman from Mexico was because she called the house."

"Anything else?"

I shook my head. "Mom was a little mad at me."

"Do you know where they found your father's car?"

"No." My voice cracked. "I didn't think he was really missing."

Tarek tilted his head. "Why not?"

"My father wasn't really a good husband." I swallowed. "If cheating on your wife was an Olympic sport, he'd win gold every time."

"Ellie." His impatience was clear as day in his voice. "Relevance?"

"He was rarely ever home. When he's not jetting off to some other country for work, he would often go missing for days with one of his little sluts. Then he'd pop up again as if nothing was wrong." I explained. "The first time he went missing, we called the cops. Three days later, they found him hold up in a hotel room with a twenty-year-old."

"I see." He pulled out his cell, scrolled then tapped. The phone must have been on speaker for I could ear it ring, and he hadn't bother lifting it to his ear.

"French." A female voice came over the line as clear as day.

Tarek cleared his throat then turned his back to face the window once more. "Maia, it's Cobra. How are you, beautiful?"

"I'd be a lot better if you're calling to book a date."

Tarek chuckled. "How about I make you a deal? If you can help me with this favour, dinner's on me."

"Oh Sugar, if it's on that delectable body..."

I almost threw up.

Tarek laughed. "Not on my body. Focus your freaky little mind for me a second, would you?"

I turned away from him then—a knife in my heart.

"Boo Tarek Jonas—you're zero fun." She teased. "How may I be of help, your highness?"

"Jeffery Sargent." Tarek continued. "Where did they find his car?" He stopped.

"Well, I'm not on that case." She paused. "But let me...outside Big Timber. As a matter of fact—the car was in a little bit of a ditch at the welcome sign."

"Interesting...think I could take a look at it?"

"It's been towed to Billings." Maia told him. "If you want in, I can make a few phone calls. I might have to escort you in, but it shouldn't be an issue. You're a cop."

"Thanks."

"Why are you looking into this, Cobra?" Maia asked. "I thought you were on vacation."

"Long story." Tarek told her. "I'll explain it all later. In the meantime, make those calls for me."

"You got it. And Cobra?"

"Mmm?"

"Watch your six, okay? If you need an extra gun..."

"You'll be my first call, my beauty."

When silence filled the room, I looked back at him.

"Get changed," he said, heading for the door. "We're going for a ride."

COBRA

SHIELDS RIVER ROAD carried us to US-89 South. During that stretch, neither of us spoke. I knew it wasn't a good idea to be in such a tight space alone with her. But I was a professional. This was work and nothing else.

In high school I hadn't been attracted to her. There was something rotten about her and for the first little while, I couldn't quite put my finger on it.

Her friend Susan on the other hand—well, how could I not be attracted? I was a teenage boy with what I thought was my type, and Susan was definitely it.

Other than the strange feelings I had around Ellie, there was something else. Ellie had been unnecessarily cruel to others, bitter and mean-spirited.

Susan had more of a brain in her head and always seemed to be sweet to those around her. The fact she was curvy helped to turn my head.

Yet, as I walked into that room and saw Ellie, I couldn't help but appreciate the look of her as an adult.

I couldn't show my attraction. There was no way she

had changed. Deep down I knew she was still that same mean little girl who terrorised our small town's high school. She was the same vindictive child who almost cost my family everything.

Though I knew it was a bad idea, I couldn't help noticing how the uncertainty of her blue eyes turned me on. The rise and fall of her breasts, the curves of her body—all of it made me hard.

But that was where it ended. She'd made it clear I wasn't good enough.

I wasn't a hard learner.

"I'm sorry." Her voice shook.

"Not interested, Ellie." I told her. "Your apology means nothing to me."

"You can't mean that."

"Can't I?" I glanced over at her then back at the road. "How many years has it been? Fifteen? Sixteen? Your sorry means nothing."

"People change, you know?"

I frowned. "Sure, for the worse. Rarely, do they ever change for the better."

"Rare, but possible."

"In your case, most likely not."

Ellie didn't speak.

The hour and a half ride to just outside Big Timber was torture. Her silence was a little unnerving because I didn't know what was happening inside her head. Thoughts swirling through my head about this entire thing left me exhausted over it all. I shouldn't ever be thinking of anything long term with Ellie Sargent. I shouldn't be craving anything carnal with her—ever.

But someone hadn't bothered telling my cock. Each time I thought of the pink of her lips and wondered if her nipples were the same colour, my entire body heated to bursting.

At the welcome sign, I pulled over and killed the engine. For a moment, I merely sat there, taking in the area, looking around for anything or anyone that would seem out of place. The place was pretty much bare. Someone had tried making the front of the sign presentable. They'd set up some lawn as well as flowers, but their hard work had been in vain. Since there hadn't been rain for weeks, the flowers were wilted, and the lawn had turned brown.

I climbed from the vehicle and closed the door but didn't cross the street. Instead, I leaned on the vehicle and waited. The air was a touch cooler and I appreciate that.

Traffic was less than light and aside from a rusted-out Honda, nothing else passed. Still, I checked both directions before jogging across the street with Ellie on my heels. I hunched down to inspect tire tracks which had dried in the mud. Those were definitely not Jeffrey's.

A piece of police tape fluttered in the breeze drawing my attention and I headed for it. Just below the sign were footprints, but I couldn't be sure whose they were. A little way down, I found blood. I stoop to check out the area with the blood and Ellie gasped.

"Is that…?"

"Blood, yes." I replied.

"A gun?" She asked.

"I'm a cop, Ellie." I signed in exasperation and without looking up at her. "We carry them around these parts."

She made an annoyed sound in her throat and I ignored it.

My inspection of the location gave me very little. I wasn't sure what I expected to find. But this wasn't it. "There must be a reason Jeffrey pulled over here."

"Maybe he was tired?" Ellie volunteered.

I pushed to my full height and looked around then focused in the direction of the town. From where I stood, I could see right down the center of it, along the main street. "Maybe." I mused. "But why here? There's nothing here. The town isn't very far from…"

The familiar ping of a bullet clanging off the metal echoed around us.

Ellie screamed.

I wrapped my arms around her and pulled her to the ground beneath my frame. We were in the open and if I didn't think of something, we were both dead.

"The actual fuck?" She screeched.

What the actual fuck is my sentiment too.

"Stay down!" I growled. "Sniper."

"No?" Ellie spat. "Really?"

I'll strangle you later.

Another bullet hit the dirt close to my head as I covered her body with mine.

"Do you have a compact?" I asked.

"Now?" Ellie snapped. "Not the right time, Tarek."

"Ellie!" I warned. "A compact—yes or no?"

She shoved her hands into her purse and removed her compact and handed it over. "What's that for?"

"Well." I opened it and after the sniper fired again and missed, I had the direction he was attacking from. "If he can't see us, he can't hit us, right?"

"Um...sure?"

I lifted my head slight, caught the sun just right and sent the reflection back into the sniper's eyes. He began firing aimlessly and I yanked Ellie off the ground.

"Stay behind me!" I ordered. "Keep up."

I moved the mirror from position to position as we hurried across the street back to our vehicle. That way, the glare would remain strong and affecting the sniper's vision. Ellie dove into the backseat of the Charger and I tossed myself behind the wheel. I didn't bother putting my seatbelt on but shoved the vehicle into drive and turned it across the open space. Close to the edge of a few trees that had their leaves dried and falling, I saw the sniper who had dropped his rifle and was now running across the empty space.

I sped up and ploughed right into him but stopped suddenly so I wouldn't crush his head. After a quick look back to ensure Ellie was okay, I scrambled out and stoop by the man's head. I pulled at the ski mask and long, dark hair spilled out.

"Son of a bitch." I growled. "A woman...who are you working for?"

Blood pooled down the sides of her mouth. She wouldn't make it very long, I knew that. I had seen this more than once. I also doubt she would do the right thing and cleared her conscience before dying. Ellie's presence filled the space beside me, and I ignored her gasp. On a hunch, I picked up the woman's right arm and rolled up the sleeve. There, tattooed to her wrist was a black and red spider with a radioactive symbol on its back. I frowned as I used my phone to take a picture of it and the woman's face.

"Tell me something." I looked up at Ellie. "Is your family's motto *go big or go home* when it comes to completely fucking up your lives?"

"Shouldn't we call 9-1-1?" Ellie ignored my question.

"Why bother?" I asked, dropping the sniper's hand to the ground. "She's going to be dead before they leave the station."

"You can't mean that?"

I leaned in close to the dying woman. "I suggest you make your peace with whatever god you pray to. Soon, you're going to have to answer for the shit you've heaped on mankind."

Her eyes bulged but I showed my irritation by standing to my full height.

"*Por favor.*" She pleaded. "*Mátame.*"

"What's she saying?" Ellie asked.

"She wants me to kill her." I translated then stooped beside her once more. "You took a shot at me, so I'm not feeling particularly charitable today."

"*Por favor!*" The woman shouted, then coughed up blood.

"At least move the car off her." Ellie pleaded.

"You might not believe this. But the car is the only thing keeping her alive right now." I wandered back to where the rifle had fallen, ejected the bullet in the chamber and carried it back to dump in my trunk. After closing it in, I went back to the woman and felt for any sign of life.

There was none.

"Let's go." I turned for the driver's side of the car.

"We can't just leave her here."

"You grew a conscience?" I demanded. "Tell me when."

"I'm getting sick of your bullshit and petty-ass comments!" Ellie shouted angrily. "You just let her die!"

"You want to switch places with her?" I asked, stalking toward her. "Because it was either you or her and in war you can' have both."

"We could have saved her."

"You keep believing that."

Ellie took a swing at me and I caught her wrist in a tight fist. "You'd better be prepared for going all in with that, Ellie. Because if you want to fight, we can fight—but I'd enjoy it."

A soft sound escaped her slightly parted lips. I could see her chest rise and fall and I wondered if my threat had turned her on. I smirked and she yanked her arm away from me and placed some distance between us.

Ellie stomped her feet. "Why is this happening!" She screamed.

"It's karma's way of paying you back for the years of wanton freedom you've enjoyed." I looked around. "Get in the car."

For another hour, I sped from Big Timber and into Billings. I pulled into the parking lot after calling the garage and thankfully, Grim was still there.

"Ellie Sargent, meet Dante McWelland," I introduced her to Grim.

"Grim," he said, while shaking her hand.

"As in Reaper?" Ellie asked.

He laughed. "Nope. Just Grim."

"Oh…" Ellie looked over at me then nodded.

"Come on in." Grim told us.

My friend led us through the checkpoints and into the area where Jeffrey's car was now parked. The first thing I noticed was that the front left tire was punctured. That would make sense as to why Jeffrey had pulled over where he had. Chances were, they'd used the sniper to take out the tire. He couldn't have driven all the way into Big Timber with it the way it was.

Grim handed me a pair of gloves and I slipped my fingers into it so I could take a closer look at the car.

"I thought you were on vacation." Grim pointed out.

"I thought so too." I opened the door and hunched down by the vehicle. "But it seems no rest for the wicked."

"Come on, Cobra." Grim pushed. "How did you get drawn into this whole thing? I mean, it came over the radio that Mrs. Sargent was killed after her husband went missing. I thought you weren't a fan of that family —no offense."

"None taken." Ellie's voice was strained with control.

"Yeah well, when they gave me that badge—they took away the choice of picking and choosing." I leaned over to sniff at the interior. "Do you smell that?"

Grim joined me at the door. "Smoke?" He sniffed again. "That's smoke—that smell wasn't there before."

"Ellie, did Jeffrey smoke?" I asked.

"No." She told me. "He didn't."

"Strange." I rose and walked around to the driver's side. I took stock of how the seat was set up. "Jeffrey was about—what? Six-foot, six foot two?"

"Sounds about right." Ellie replied.

"Someone else was using the seat." I pointed out. "Someone shorter. I'm guessing no prints?"

"Not even his prints. Which means someone wiped down the inside." Grim pressed his lips into a line. "This car is basically a dud."

"Okay...so now we know why he pulled over where he did."

"Basically, it was an ambush." Grim mused. "From the blood in the car, we know he was hurt—enough to be bleeding."

"They tested it?" I asked.

"Yeah. Got the results back this morning." Grim shrugged. "Maia had them put a rush on it."

I invited Grim out for lunch with us and after picking up enough food for the three of us, I drove them to my place. Grim and I checked the house then sat down to call Taz, Montana and Swede on video chat.

"What you're saying is, there isn't enough blood in the car to say he's dead?" Ellie asked.

I nodded. "Precisely. I think they took out his tire to make him pull over. There must have been a struggle and in order to get him out of the vehicle, they had to hurt him."

Ellie winced.

"Any idea who *they* are?" Grim asked while shoving a fry into his mouth.

"A sniper took a shot at us at the Big Timber sign." I confided while pouring myself some scotch.

"What?" Montana asked. "Are you alright?"

"We're still standing." Ellie replied.

"Okay." Swede cut in. "You keep saying, they. Are we any closer in finding out who *they* are?"

I set my drink on the table and found the picture I had taken of the sniper's wrist and turned it to the screen.

"You've got to be kidding!" Taz said.

"Araña Tóxica," Montana muttered. "Well, shit."

"When the Sargents fuck up." I picked up my drink. "They do it big."

I sat, leaned back in the seat and closed my eyes. No one spoke. It seemed there had been an unwritten rule —survive a sniper, you deserve some peace to contemplate the fragility of mortality.

Someone cleared their throat and I sat up.

"Okay," Ellie said. "I'm going to ask. What's Araña Tóxica?"

"It seems." Montana began. "Your father has managed to piss off Colombia's biggest drug cartel. Now they want to wipe every trace of him off the face of the planet."

"How do you know that?" Ellie asked.

Taz was next to speak. "The picture Cobra showed us is of a tattoo—only the Araña Tóxica has that tattoo on their right wrist. There is a saying from the bible that they use—*si tu mano derecha te ofende, la cortas.*"

"I…" Ellie looked over at me. "I don't speak Spanish —that's Spanish, right?"

"It means—roughly, if your right hand offends you, chop it off." I explained.

"Wait—they don't really—well, cut off the hands of those who goes against them, right?" Ellie wanted to know. She looked from Grim to the guys on the screen.

"The Araña Tóxica is dangerous." Grim spoke up. "They've been known to cut out tongues—and they have chopped off a few right arms. They are brutal. The fact your father pissed them off will not end well. So, we're going to need you to think *real* hard."

"I don't know anything about Colombia or this gang." Ellie stressed. "Dad never discussed business— not with me anyway. He is—er was always saying shit like, *it's need to know.*"

I frowned. "They'll just keep coming."

"I agree." Montana agreed. "We're going to have to find out where they're sourced and take that out."

"What about my father?" Ellie asked. "I mean, if you take out wherever they are, he could die."

I rose and finished my drink. "If God's merciful, he's already dead."

ELLIE

THE MOMENT I woke up that morning, I kept wishing the last few days had been a horrible nightmare. But as I awoke in a strange bed with unusual air and walls around me, I knew it was no figment of a dream world.

My mother was dead, and my father was missing.

Tarek Jonas was my protector and he was very unwilling.

I reluctantly climbed out of bed, showered and dressed in a black dress I had grabbed when the Protectors came to my aid. It was handy when I was frantically shoving things into the little bag I'd managed to yank out of my closet. Thankfully, it seemed appropriate for a funeral, but I didn't feel like burying anyone that day.

As I walked through the cemetery to where my mother would be laid to rest, I was flanked by Kujo and Tarek's friend, Maia.

The moment I met her, I knew why I didn't stand a chance at turning Tarek's head. She was gorgeous—with long black hair tied up in a sensible ponytail. Her dark eyes sized me up with silent contemplation. leaving me feeling uneasy and invisible. But it didn't stop there. Maia had flawless caramel skin wrapped in curves that could make the sexiest supermodel jealous and a grown man cry.

Yes, I felt like an insignificant ogre next to her.

Every time I think about her, I thought of Pocahontas wrapped in John Rambo. Then she hunched down to tie the laces of her combat boot and I caught sight of her badge and gun.

I had to laugh.

Of course.

As we approached the area for my mother's burial, I tucked my jealousy to the very back of my mind and focused. I didn't really have a choice in where I buried my mom. The funeral was planned in two hours for the next day. Although I realized I had been an asshole to the people around me, even I recognized my mother was worth more than a few shitty hours.

But I didn't have a choice.

My life had imploded, and I couldn't seem to go anywhere without bullets flying.

I hadn't cried for my mother after she died. Her murder did hurt but I was pretty sure I deserved that pain. To say I was unsure of how to take it all must be the understatement of the year.

"What's wrong?" Maia asked.

"What?"

"You keep looking around." Maia didn't look at me. "Is something wrong?"

"I just thought he'd be here. That's all."

"Cobra?"

I nodded.

"Just because you don't see him, doesn't mean he's not here."

I wouldn't have been offended if Tarek hadn't come. It would suck but I would have understood. Everyone else I called said they would attend but so far, not one of them had bothered showing up. My friends, Jennifer and Susan had cut off all communications with me after the murder and I was basically left to deal.

In fact, I was pretty sure Susan had changed her number. I tried checking them out on Facebook and to my horror, it seemed they had me blocked.

These two women were supposed to be my best friends.

The thought made me sad. She'd spent her entire life with my father and his people. All hers were left by the wayside and after a while, they stopped caring. It wasn't their faults. Life got in the way.

That, and my father had systematically eliminated everyone from her world until all she had was him.

We got settled to one side of the casket. Atop it were yellow roses—my mother's favorite.

I wrapped my arms around myself and hung my head. It was hard to breathe. The stifling air around me wasn't doing me any favours either. It pushed into my lungs as seconds morphed into minutes then into dim pulse of the silent past.

My mother was barely in her sixties—how could she be gone?

The pastor prattled on and on about coming from

dust and going back there. He tossed some dirt atop the coffin while mumbling about ashes and dust. When he finished, he walked over to shake my hand, offer his condolences then left us standing there. As the lone worker cranked the wench to lower the coffin into the grave, I stepped forward to lay my flower on the top of the others and Kujo and Maia gave me a moment alone with her.

Time ticked by.

The breeze drifted through the leaves on the tree sending them swirling around to the ground.

"I got her!" The urgency in Maia's voice was palpable.

Before I could react, Maia gripped my arm, pulled me into her chest and spun. Something smashed into the tree beside me, but it wasn't until Maia's gun roared in response did I even realize someone was shooting at us.

"This is a funeral!" I shrieked. "The actual fuck is wrong with people?"

A bullet flew over my head and Maia pushed me toward her black jeep.

"Kujo!" I called.

"I'm okay!" He replied over the bullets. "Go with Maia."

I tripped over an outcropped root but caught myself on a nearby angel. Soon, I was herded away and to the jeep.

Maia handled her gun like a pro, protecting me. I dove into the back of the vehicle and slammed the door closed behind me.

"Get in the back!" I screamed, climbing between the seats and starting the engine. When I looked around to her, and saw Maia in, I shoved the car into drive and climbed the curb.

"Where are you going?" Maia asked.

"Kujo!" I replied. "We can't leave him here."

The jeep rattled over cobblestones, tree roots and knocked over a tombstone.

"Sorry!" I squealed but didn't stop to fix it. I pulled the jeep between Kujo and the shooters, keeping my head down. "Kujo! Get in!"

Once he was in, I sped off toward the road once more, rattling over uneven ground. I drove across the sidewalk narrowly missing a lady who screamed and gave me the finger. "Sorry!" I hollered just as the jeep bounced off the edge so fast, the front made a god-awful sound against the asphalt.

I wasn't sure where I was going, but I had to pull over as my hands were shaking. My eyes blurred with tears.

"Shit." I muttered and shoved out of the jeep. "My mother's funeral! Is nothing sacred!"

"Ellie." Kujo caught my shoulders. "Get in the car."

"It's hard to breathe." I told him.

"I know, sweetie." Kujo rubbed his palms up and down my arms. "But we have to go just in case we're being followed."

When I climbed into the back, Maia checked my eyes, pulse and skin. I figured she was trying to see if I was about to pass out or something to that effect. We drove back to the ranch and I flopped into the sofa.

"Drink this."

I looked up to see Maia was pressing a crystal glass into my hand. Without bothering to check what it was, I knocked it back and instantly regretted it. The liquid burned a trail down my throat to warm my belly. "What's this?"

"Scotch." Maia tipped her head back and drained hers. "It's not everyday you have to bury your mother then have the funeral turn into a shootout."

I managed another sip. She had a point. "Where's Kujo?"

"Went to pick up the King."

"Who?"

"Cobra?" She arched a brow at me. "As in, King Cobra?"

I drained my glass and winced. "Oh."

I MUST HAVE PASSED OUT. Though I was a party girl, the hard stuff wasn't my thing. But Maia had been right, the day called for something a little stronger than expensive wines.

A soft sigh escaped my lips.

I dreamt of Tarek Jonas. In my fantasy, he was in love with me. He looked at me the way a lover should, touched me like I thought he was always meant to.

When I opened my eyes again, there was a blanket over me and the standing lamp beside me was on. A dog was curled up in front of the sofa.

I missed Lilah then.

Most mornings, I would wake to her curled into the

sheet between my ass and legs. Though I scolded her that I could squish her, I secretly enjoyed it. When I shifted, the dog lifted its head and barked. Tarek entered with a mug.

"You're awake," he said, handing me the cup.

It wasn't easy to make my mind behave. The t-shirt he wore fell perfectly against his toned torso leaving very little to the imagination. At some point during his time away from Eagle Rocks, Tarek had gotten so muscular and sexy, every time I thought about him, I grew wet.

That wasn't normal.

"The dog?" I thanked him with a silent toast. "Is he yours"

Tarek hunched down to scratch the pooch behind the ears. "Good boy. Good boy!" He cooed. "No, not mine. This fantastic beast is Kujo's partner. His name is Six."

"He's cute."

"And smart. Right boy?"

Six barked happily, wagged his tail and nipped at Tarek's hand. Instead of being angry, Tarek merely leaned forward and kissed the German Sheppard's head. Six yawned widely then batted at Tarek's hand playfully while squirming in happiness.

"Is Kujo here?"

"No. After you all but passed out, he came by. Six knew something was wrong. He wouldn't leave you and Kujo knew better than to try forcing him." Tarek explained. "War dogs—they are smarter than most."

"Oh. My own little guardian angel."

Six licked at Tarek's chin. I didn't think he could get any sexier but watching the way he interacted with the dog, did my heart well. Six rolled over for Tarek to scratch his belly caused Tarek to laugh.

It broke me. He'd never laugh like that for me—he wouldn't even smile.

"We need to talk." The business in Tarek's voice drew me back to reality. "Come on."

I hesitated. Just because I had to leave my happy place, didn't mean I wanted to. Still, I followed him down the hall to an office. There was paper all over the desk, pictures pinned to a white board and red tacks in a large map on the far wall.

"The Araña Tóxica is a gang out of Colombia." He began. "Sit down."

I fell into the only empty chair available. All the others were loaded with paperwork.

"They became known for murdering every known member of a rival gang and taking over the lead for heroine out of the Comuna 13 in Colombia. Comuna 13 is one of the most dangerous slums in the country and from there, they traffic the stuff into the United States." Tarek pointed to a picture of a man who looked like a Tele-Novella reject. "This is Otis Valentina. He's in charge. The DEA has been trying to nab him for years. No luck."

"Okay." I inhaled, held the breath then pushed it out my nose and mouth at the same time. "I'm assuming you're telling me this because he's the one after me. The question I have right now—why?"

"That we don't know." Tarek pointed to a timeline

with missing pieces. "While you slept, I've been trying to piece together your father's life over the last two years or so. These spots we have no idea where he was or what he was up to. Can you add anything?"

I approached the board and studied it. "This one, I remember it was around my birthday. I remember my mom planned this huge party, but we couldn't get a hold of him."

"Okay."

"Um…" I followed the trail. "This one, he claimed he had a conference in Billings and couldn't be disturbed. We thought he was working. All the others, no clue. My father wasn't a very forthcoming man with his time."

Tarek stared at the timeline. "Your father has pissed off a drug cartel. We don't really know how. But from what you've told me about his penchant for different women and secrets, I'm going to go out on a line in assuming he either slept with the boss' woman or messed with is product."

"Product? Do you mean drugs."

"Yes."

"Well." I rubbed my palms into my thighs. "I've never seen my father high or anything like that. Then again, I'm beginning to realize I don't know him at all, so who knows?"

Silence.

"Ellie, what you did for Kujo and Maia…"

"It was the least I could do." I swallowed the rising lump in my throat. "Maia means something to you. It doesn't take a genius to figure that out. The last thing I need right now is for her to get hurt because of me."

"Maia can take care of herself."

"I'm aware of that." I said it a little too harshly and immediately caught myself. "I'm hungry. Are you hungry?"

He sighed. "There's some stew on the stove and rice in the cooker. Help yourself."

I all but ran from the room. It was bad enough I was having nightmares about him letting me die to save Maia. I didn't need to hear him praise her bad-ass *fantasticness* too.

I knew he could never forgive me. But that didn't stop me from wanting.

COBRA

SEEING the Crazies in front of me heading into Big Timber always grounded me. They overpowered every feeling I had, leaving me free, leaving me with a new appreciation of things in the world greater than me.

I had been battling my emotions and the lustful thoughts Ellie sent through me. They weren't her fault, yet I had spent most of the ride angry at her for making me want her. I couldn't do anything about what I had raging through me—I didn't want to let Malik down or disappoint my parents.

Besides, I was still angry at her and I could have gone right on feeling as if she caused the end of my world had the Protectors not guilted me into helping her. Then again, I could have transferred her case to Maia, or called in one of my guys, like Grim to handle it. As a matter of fact, I should have done one of those alternatives. I wouldn't have to be around her, and my life could have gone on being mine.

But I hadn't and it was too late to turn back. Keeping

her safe was the right thing to do and my parents would kick my ass if I hadn't done what was right.

I sighed.

Having her so close forced me to face the fact I wanted to feel the sharp bite of her nails in my flesh. I wanted to listen to her breath speed up and feel it wash over my skin. I wanted to spank her, to pull her hair.

I wanted to fuck her like she deserved.

It wasn't easy pushing those thoughts from my mind or keeping them from making me hard. The thought of being unprofessional wrapped its way around them and the battle continued. I was a cop and my duty to Ellie Sargent was to keep her safe, find her father and put the bad guys either in their graves or a six by eight cell.

Once that was over, I'd go back to my life and let her go on with hers. Maybe I should take Grim up on his offer to set me up. He'd tried for a few years and I always declined. After a while, he stopped offering.

I glanced over at her to the way her hair fluttered in the wind and wondered if it would smell like roses or some other delicious scent I couldn't resist. I wondered if she liked her men forceful and strong or gentle.

I sighed.

The thoughts plagued me until I parked behind a local diner sitting beside an abandoned house. The last time we parked in the open, we had a sniper taking pot-shots at us. I wasn't about to take any chances. Without looking over at her, I climbed from the front seat of the car and stretched my back.

"You okay?" Ellie asked.

"Fine." I told her. "My back's been throbbing a little, that's all."

"Maybe we should leave this for another time."

I shook my head. "We're already here. And besides, the sooner we can get some insight on what's really going on, the sooner we can end this."

She didn't seem convinced, but I started walking around the building just in case she began asking any further questions. Ellie joined me and I stopped to ensure my coat was around my gun and badge. The last thing I needed was to announce my status as a cop. People were much more likely to speak to me if they believed I was one of them.

Malik said I had a trusting face.

The moment they realized I carried a badge—well, no more information was usually forthcoming then.

Together we entered the diner, a tiny bell jangled over our heads. The moment we stepped though the door, the conversations dropped to a minimal. Wasn't surprising.

I pressed my palm to the small of Ellie's back and kind of eased her toward a table rather than allowing her to bring us to a booth. The place was small but had a healthy crowd. People stared openly but I picked up the menu. I wasn't reading it. Instead I was taking in the place as much as I could. I had already clocked the exits and routes for the fastest get-a-way.

"What can I get you?"

I set the menu down and smiled up at her. She was pregnant—very pregnant. "Coffee, black—please?"

She grinned. "And for you, miss?"

"Coffee, milk, no sugar. And that ham and cheese looks really good." Ellie told her.

After the waitress left, I watched her go then leaned forward to speak with Ellie. "Always know where your exits are." I told her. "What's the quickest way out. Learn your surroundings, the people inside of it."

"I'm not a soldier."

"No. But this could save your life." I told her. "Since we arrived, the man at the end of the bar has made two phone calls."

"So?" She turned her head to me, but I knew she was watching the man from the corner of her eyes. "He's staring—who'd he call?"

"We're about to find out."

"Shouldn't we leave?"

I shrugged as the waitress brought the coffee and I thanked her. When she left, I glanced out the glass window. "IF we leave, we get nothing and will draw attention to ourselves. It's going to take a while for them to bring the sandwich."

"It doesn't take that long to make a—right, to buy time."

I nodded, proud of her. "In the meantime, keep your eyes on me and prepare to move."

"At least we know something more now."

"What's that?"

"My father was here," Ellie replied. "If he wasn't, I doubt they'd know to expect us."

I smiled. Ellie was smarter than I gave her credit for.

It didn't take twenty minutes to make a sandwich. It was actually offensive they thought I wouldn't catch on to what was happening. It didn't take long for two motorcycles to pull up and parked hurriedly in the lot.

"They're here," I said. "Come and sit beside me."

When she did, I shifted in my chair and pulled her into my chest. I needed her close when it came time to move. Still, I waited by cradling one of her cheek with my palm and lifted her lips to mine. My free hand already had my gun out, using her body to mask the weapon. From the corner of my eyes I could see the newcomers. They exchanged a slight look with the man at the end of the bar who returned the nod and they made their way toward us.

When they were close enough, I dropped Ellie's cheek, used that hand to propel her to her feet while shifting to aim at them. The first man took a bullet to the foot. He screamed but I wasn't focused on him. I found Ellie just as she tossed her hot coffee in the other man's face and we took off for the door.

The man who was sitting at the bar hopped over his fallen friend and I could hear his footsteps heaving behind us. Outside the back door, I tugged Ellie to the wall behind me and waited for our pursuer to exit. Once he did, I sent a high kick to his chest and he slammed backward into the door just as it closed. He gasped but I didn't wait for him to react before following it up with another kick.

The man slumped to his knees then face first into the dirt. Ellie ran over.

"Is he dead?" She asked.

"Not yet." I growled.

Eventually, I got him into the trunk and drove him

out of town. When we arrived at a desolate area, I pulled over.

"We're stopping?" She asked. "Why?"

"Our friend and I are about to have a conversation." I relied.

"You're not going to kill him, are you?"

I shrugged nonchalantly. "It depends."

"On?"

"What he has to say. And if he lies to me or not." I told her simply as I climbed from the car. When I opened the truck, he tried running. I caught him by the back of the neck to stop his retreat, pulled him out and shoved him to his knees.

"Let's talk." I growled.

"I know who sent you." I glanced up to Ellie—but only for a second. The question is, why."

"Fuck you."

I smiled. "If it was up to me, you'd already be dead. But see that woman? For some reason she doesn't want you dead. She seems to think you can be redeemed. Me? I'm an asshole. I think you're done and there's no going back. So, prove one of us right—I don't particularly care which."

The man looked over at Ellie and I slapped him against the back of the head.

"Hey! Focus on the one with the gun." I warned. "Now, I believe my question is a very simple one. Why."

Silence.

The last fuck I had to give dissipated along with my last nerve.

"Okay." I pushed the gun into my holster and

grabbed him. I tugged him to the car and bent him over the hood while twisting his arm dangerously backward.

"They'll kill me!" He squealed.

"And what the fuck do you think I'm going to do to you?" I snarled.

"But you said…"

"Yeah, that went out the window." I twisted his arm even more making him scream. "What happens to you now, is totally up to me. So, here's the deal."

I dug his wallet out and found his license then tossed it behind me. "Okay Sam, is it okay if I call you Sam? Or do you prefer to go by Samuel? Oh, well, it doesn't matter. Listen, Sam. I'm about to let you go. Then, I'm going to hit one of the Araña Tóxica hideouts and while there, I'm going to announce it at the top of my lungs how helpful, you've been. And trust me, Sam, I got a big mouth."

"I didn't tell you shit!" Samuel tried pushing away.

I only ramped up the pressure on his arm.

"But do you really think it's going to matter?" I asked. "They hear you were in the same zip code as a US Marshal and they shoot first and ask questions later."

"Shit." Samuel grunted.

"Ah—language. There's a lady present. I'm not going to ask you again."

Samuel grumbled something. "He slept with Valentina's sister…"

"Who?" Ellie asked.

"Your old man." Samuel replied. "Got her pregnant then made off with a good chuck of Valentina's product. I'm talking millions of dollars worth of the good stuff."

"The hell does that have to do with me?" Ellie stepped forward.

"You're his kid." Samuel spat. "Valentina believes you know where the stash is. Even if you don't, they're hoping if they can get their hands on you, they'll be able to squeeze your old man till he talks."

"This is dumb." Ellie eyed him. "I'm not apart of any of this."

"Man, does she have to be your stereotypical blond?" Samuel sighed. "It doesn't matter. Your father soiled his sister, which in his head meant he had to kill her—Otis, I mean. In his head, your entire family is at fault."

"Is this guy for real?" Ellie asked.

"Unfortunately, that's how the Araña Tóxica thinks." I confirmed.

I watched Ellie carefully as she moved even closer, her eyes burning a hole through Samuel. "Where's the kid now?" She asked.

But Sam only laughed with insanity bright in his eyes. "You actually think you can stop what's coming?" He actually had the nerve to sound incredulous. "This entire situation has been years in the making. It's a fucking runaway train—you can't stop it."

I shoved Samuel away from us and he tumbled to the ground. Instead of scampering away, he merely rolled from side to side laughing harder.

"Get in the car." I told Ellie.

"What..."

"Get in the car!" I barked.

"You can't stop it!" Samuel hollered. "As for the kid,

hopefully he was merciful and bashed his head in with a rock!"

"Let me bash his head in with a rock!" Ellie growled while trying to get out of the vehicle.

I locked the door and turned on the engine. "It doesn't matter. Even if he leaves here alive, he's a dead man."

ELLIE

THE PROTECTORS and Tarek had a meeting to discuss what was happening and what we found out. Though I was there, it was as if I was millions of miles away. I couldn't seem to focus on anything they said because I was still back with Samuel, hearing that I had a possible brother or sister that could be dead.

Did my mother know? Did she know that he refused to have another child with her but had gone out and had a kid with someone else who led to her death? How could I reconcile my father with that information—with those actions?

How could he?

…And Tarek had kissed me.

I covered my face with my hands.

"Okay." Tarek was saying. "We'll head back tomorrow. But for tonight, we should stop and just breathe."

It didn't take long for the house to clear out and I exhaled long and hard. Tarek's presence filled the room and my body trembled. The thought of his mouth on mine returned to me and every bit of me wanted—needed—to happen again.

I didn't dare look up. The last thing I needed was another reason for him to see just how weak I was. As I tried walking by him, he caught my arm and pulled me into his chest. No, this wasn't how it was supposed to be. Not after what I'd done.

I tried fighting him—to get out of his embrace but he held on tighter. Tarek pressed a large palm to the back of my head as the tears finally fell.

"You can't." I sobbed. "You shouldn't be comforting me like this."

"Shh." Tarek hushed me. "You've been through a lot. Most people would be down by now. You're still standing."

"This is my punishment."

"I'm pretty sure that's not how it works." His voice was soft.

For the first time ever, I was home. I was the one who belonged in Tarek's arms, under his body, in his bed. But what kind of waste of space did It make me, lusting after another woman's man?

If only I had acted right—Tarek could have been mine. I could have been the one he called beautiful and wanted to be around. But I had ruined that. I broke his heart and now he had someone else.

I cried harder.

I know I didn't deserve peace. Still, I allowed myself to accept the little I could get. I would give Maia her man back, once the shaking stopped.

Tarek scooped me into his arms and carried me to the sofa. Once he had the blanket up to my shoulders, he sat on the edge of the couch and pushed a strand of hair from my forehead.

"Ellie." He exhaled. "How did it get this bad?"

"I'm not sure." I sighed. My eyes fluttered closed. I knew words left my lips. I felt them seep out and into the universe. When I forced my eyes open, Tarek stared down at me with an unfamiliar expression.

I trembled.

"I-I'm sorry." I managed.

…Then the sandman came.

He didn't stay long. My nightmares had been too strong. They burgeon their way into my brain and forced me awake with a start. I was alone and it had gotten darker. Still tired, I pulled the blanket off, stuck my feet out and hurried to the bathroom. I washed my face and tried looking at least a little presentable before I went searching for Tarek.

I found him standing at the desk, palms braced to it while reading from a laptop. What caused my breath to catch in my throat was the fact he was shirtless. Suddenly, I couldn't breathe.

My feet carried me across the space, and I pressed my palm to his back. His body was hard and warm—just as I'd dreamed.

Tarek turned to look at me over one shoulder.

The look in his eyes should have terrified me. It was heated like a wild beast ready to devour his prey. But I wanted to be his prey. I wanted to endure every bit of his ardour I could get. Instead of backing away, I wrapped my arms around his body and dragged my palm down his toned abs to his belt. When he didn't stop me, I slid one hand down into his pants while pushing to my tiptoes and bit his neck.

Tarek swirled, caught me by the throat and shoved me across the room until my back stopped against the wall. He breathed hard, hot breath bathed my face as he moved his mouth down to the side of my face. Having his large palm at my throat turned me on. My nipples tightened and I whimpered.

"I've warned you before, Ellie." Tarek grounded out. "You need to be prepared to go all in. You have no idea what you're playing with."

I dug my nails into his sides, and he growled. He bit my earlobe and I grunted then moaned as he sucked on the spot beneath my ear. Before I could enjoy what he was doing to me, Tarek lifted his head and dropped his mouth on mine. The kiss was raw, wild and I wanted more. My brain screamed with happiness that didn't have time to explode out my mouth. He shoved his tongue into my mouth, pressed his body into mine and used his free hand to tug at my shorts.

Yes!

Yes!

Please?

There were no doubts left—I wanted Tarek. He was the right kind of monster to give me what I needed, to take away the softness I had always gotten in bed. He was the only man to use my body like I deserved. I needed that—I needed him.

But before I could show him how desperately I

wanted him, Tarek released me and backed up, his shoulders rising and falling. The darkness in his eyes called to me. When I reached for him again, Tarek backed away and stormed from the room.

"Tarek!" I called.

The only response I received, was his footsteps thundering up the stairs followed by a slam of a door.

Weak from what he'd done to me, from being on the brink of what would no doubt be one of the most powerful orgasms I'd ever have, I slipped to my knees. It was hard to catch my breath, to get my body to cool down. I struggled to my feet and hurried into the kitchen and opened the fridge and shoved my face in.

NEITHER OF US discussed what had happened. Though I knew we probably should, I remained mute on it. I should have felt bad but all I felt was disappointed it hadn't gone further. While the house fell silent for the night, I spent the entire night trying to plan a way to get him in my arms again. But by the time the sun rose and Kujo stopped by to bring us breakfast and snacks for the road, I had nothing.

While Kujo and Tarek spoke, I cuddled Six. I missed Lilah terribly and Six was the next best thing. I rolled a ball across the floor for the German Sheppard who ran for it, caught it in his mouth and brought it back. I giggled and rubbed his head before doing it again.

When it was time to leave, I hugged Six then climbed into the passenger seat of the Nissan GTR and pulled on my belt. Kujo stopped by my window to tapped me gently on the nose. I smiled at him.

"You'll be okay," he said. "Cobra is good people."

"I know."

"Even if he doesn't like you." Kujo smirked.

"You suck at pep-talks." I teased.

"But I mean well." Kujo shrugged. "Besides, you gatta like me cause I'm adorable."

I laughed.

Kujo gave me a mock salute and whistled. Six came running and sat by his leg. Tarek got in the car beside me and instantly started the ignition. After a honk from Tarek and a wave from Kujo, we hit the road.

The journey back to Billings was simple enough. I slept the entire way. Partway there, a black Rubicon pulled in behind us just as Tarek's phone rang. He answered it on speaker phone, and it was Maia.

"Hello handsome." Maia's voice filled the vehicle. "Care for an escort?"

"Always." Tarek replied. "Swing around."

The vehicle swung wide to the lane on our right then in front of us. When the Rubicon hung a left onto a dirt road, Tarek did the same. We followed her for another ten minutes then pulled into the front yard of a beautiful ranch house. Maia stopped and climbed from the jeep, looking more like Lara Croft than any woman had a right to. She pulled a black bag from the back as Tarek and I approached her. The two hugged and she greeted me with a lift of her chin.

The moment we stepped inside, Tarek's phone rang,

and he excused himself to take it. Maia handed me the bag and though shocked, I accepted it.

"Hopefully, these fit." Maia told me. "I know you haven't had a chance to go home.

I arched a brow. "You bought me clothes?"

"It's not much." Maia shrugged. "But I figured it would—"

I burst into tears.

"Um…" Maia patted my shoulder. "It's okay. This won't be forever. You'll get to go home soon."

"I'm a horrible person." I blubbered. "You're being so nice to me and I've been dreaming about your boyfriend. I'm so sorry."

"Um—wait, what?"

"I know!"

"Ellie—who are you talking about here?"

I frowned. "Tarek."

"Wait—you think Cobra and I…" She doubled over laughing.

"It's not funny!" I shouted. "I feel bad enough and you're not helping."

"The King and I are just friends. Don't use me as an excuse." She laughed harder.

I buried my face in my hands. My life had gotten much worse. How was that even possible. "Fuck my life."

"Don't worry about it." Maia chuckled. "You're not the first person to believe Cobra and I are an item. Trust me, you won't be the last. If you're interested, you should tell him."

"Oh, no." I picked up the bag and headed for the door. "I can't."

Maia followed and we both climbed the stairs. It dawned on me then I had no idea where Tarek wanted me to sleep that night. Instead of just picking a room, I sat on the top step while Maia took the one below me.

"Why not?" She pushed.

"Haven't you been paying attention?" I wanted to know. "He hates me. The only reason he's helping me is because his badge is forcing him."

"I don't think so."

"You didn't rip his heart out and backed a dump truck over it." I rubbed my eyes. Suddenly I was more tired than I'd ever had been. "I was a stupid, *stupid*, child. I was jealous and stupid—did I say that one already?"

"A few times, yes."

"I saw him dancing with another girl." I cleared my throat. "I knew she was going to ask him out and it made me so angry. The rage that night—I couldn't remember ever feeling that pissed off, ever."

"You had a crush on our snake?"

"Not an excuse. I was a miserable, little shit."

"What exactly did you do?" Maia asked.

Before I had a chance to answer, Tarek appeared at the foot of the stairs.

"Well." He called up. "There's bad news and more bad news."

I groaned. "Of course."

"What's the bad news?" Maia asked.

"Malik wants to come over." Tarek replied.

"And the more bad news?" Maia inquired.

I didn't care, really. Bad news was only going to come back to haunt me. Still, I beat Tarek to the reply. "He couldn't stop Malik from coming over."

"Ding, ding, ding!" Tarek replied pointing at me. "Give the woman a cookie!"

"Wait—I don't get it." Maia looked from me to Tarek. "Why is this a bad thing? Oh, wait. Wow. What *did* you do?"

I shrunk back against the step then stood. "I'm going to need a place to hide."

Tarek sighed and climbed the stairs toward me. "I'll show you your room." Tarek stopped to pick up the bag Maia had given me.

Maia said nothing and Tarek led me down the corridor to a beautifully male room. If my life wasn't in danger and Tarek didn't dislike me so much, I would have taken a chance to enjoy the space. Tarek set the bag on the bed and I knew if I sat, my chest would explode. "He's not going to be happy to see me."

Tarek walked over to the window to shove the curtains aside. "No," he replied.

"And I don't suppose saying I'm sorry will change his mind?"

Tarek shook his head.

"I didn't think so." I signed and sat on the chest at the foot of the bed. "I don't even know why I reacted that way. It was never like I could have been good enough for you. You weren't wealthy, but I was never…" I rubbed my eyes. "I saw you with her and I—shit. I lost my mind I knew she'd asked you out and from the way she held you, I knew you'd said yes. I knew I wasn't—I'd like to be alone now."

To stress my point, I climbed to the bed and rolled away from him. For so long, I thought I had it all. I thought, even though my parents annoyed me, I had money. Any trouble I had could go away if I threw enough money at it. As my world burnt around me, I realized what I felt for Tarek was the only real thing. He was the only good and real thing in my entire world.

Tears seeped from my eyes and the frustration only made things worse. My body rocked with sobs. At some point, I must have fallen asleep because soon the darkness descended over my world. The nightmare came like a sharp knife slicing through my brain. My mother stood in front of me with fire and damnation in her eyes.

"Shame!" She yelled at me.

I covered my ears for her voice was loud enough to make my ears hurt.

"You should be ashamed!" She stressed.

"Please!" I screamed, trying to run but only tripped over myself and hit the ground hard. "No! Stop it!"

I screamed.

"Ellie!"

Arms grabbed my shoulders and shook.

"Ellie! Wake up."

I opened my eyes to look into unfamiliar eyes. For a moment, I struggled against his touch, panic filling my brain.

"Ellie! It's Malik." The person informed me. "It's Malik—you're okay."

I blinked and stared at him. His brown eyes were sorry, but I eased from his arms and scrambled away from him. Light floated through the curtains and I blinked again. "What time is it?"

Malik stood from the bed and checked his Rolex. "Just after nine in the morning."

"Where's Tarek?"

"He went out." Malik headed for the door. "Wash up and get dressed. He'll be back soon, and breakfast is ready."

I let him go. It was strange to see Malik Jonas. But time seemed as it had been kind to him.

When I made an appearance, Malik said nothing. He merely set a place with scrambled eggs, sausages and toast in front of me.

"If you want coffee..." His voice raspy.

"I'll get it. Thank you."

When he didn't speak again, I wandered off for coffee then sat back at the island. Though I picked up my fork, I wasn't as hungry as I should have been first thing in the morning. Malik kept on cooking and I stared at his back. He was a little more muscular than Tarek, slightly taller and he seemed a little more poised.

The silence was maddening for it was only interrupted by the sound of frying.

"Not hungry?" Malik asked.

I hadn't noticed he'd moved. I lifted my head and offered a one shoulder shrug. "You shouldn't be kind to me."

Malik arched his brow. "Why is that?"

"Come on. You know why."

Malik turned off the stove, covered the food he'd made and sat across from me. "It's hard not being right-eously pissed off at you. People see me and then Tarek's skin colour and think I have no right to be angry at what you've done. But he's my brother. And I don't give a damn about his skin colour. I would move heaven and hell to make sure he's safe."

I nodded.

"He's been alone for a long time." Malik explained. "He says he's okay. I want to believe him. But after you, I know he's afraid he'll find another you and this time, it could kill him. He's been staying alone because he's afraid history will repeat itself."

"I'm sorry." I croaked.

Malik sucked his teeth. "Tarek says to behave."

"Just tell me!"

"You ruined my family." Malik told her. "You broke my brother and you took everything. You don't ever do that again because you take away from the real victims."

"I know." I pushed the plate away.

"Then why?"

"It doesn't matter."

"It does to me!" He told me. "Tell me why."

"I was losing him. It's a fucked-up thing to have done but I thought—I thought if I couldn't have him, no one else could."

Malik arched a brow. "Wait—you had a thing for Tarek?"

"Has." I picked up a piece of toast. Confessions always made me hungry. "Present tense. I don't know how I thought that would end. I saw him with Susan and the first thing out of my mouth—I know it was wrong."

"Accusing someone of rape, Ellie."

"I know." I sobbed. "And you and your family have no reason to forgive me."

Malik exhaled.

I drew my plate closer and filled my mouth.

COBRA

THE WATER FLOWED over my body. I lifted my face to the downpour loving the feeling of the stream on my skin. But soon the flow of liquid became Ellie's fingertips trailing over my body. The smell of her hair came back to me, the softness of her skin and the singe of her breath against my skin. Her breasts had been perfect, pressing into my chest, the flesh of her throat supple and soft in my hands.

She hadn't fought me off. Instead, she'd sunk her nails into my flesh and opened up her body to me in ways my ex never had. She wanted it—every bit of the roughness I had given her. My cock perked to life at the thought of her so willing and I wanted to cry. But I knew I couldn't walk out of the bathroom with that kind of problem. Instead, I gave in to the thoughts of her and wrapped my fingers around my dick.

I turned and pressed my back to the wall, stuck my hips out and dragged my free hand up and down my abs while stroking myself. My eyes drifted closed as I saw

Ellie in front of me—naked and perfect. I yearned to taste her nipples to feel them tightened on my tongue, to hear the sounds she made while I sucked on them to my heart's content. Did she like it from behind? Would she relish in having my palms on her ass-cheeks marking her as my very own?

My body burned because of her. I writhed under my own hands, stroking tighter, faster. The pounding of my heart threatening to burst through my ears. My chest heaved with the way my breathing exploded from my body. I knew my entire world could descend into a kind of madness only she could save me from.

I'd kissed her, felt the rush of her body powerless under mine. Somehow, I was able to cage the crazed idiot running amok inside me. She did that—her body, her smell, her taste.

I pinched at my own nipples, massaged the hurt away and growled at the beautiful sensations now flickering through me like the flames of a candle.

"Ellie…" I tugged on my cock harder, trying hard to last longer, to fight off the orgasm that I knew was coming. I edged myself, pushing until I almost lost my mind then backed off. I released myself and trailed a finger against the head, smearing it in pre-cum. "Shit."

I wanted her mouth on me. Just imagining her on her knees in front of me, her blue eyes wide as I pushed to the back of her throat, carried me on again to another brink. My abs tightened and once more I stopped myself from climaxing.

Soon, it became too much. My body trembled, not from the shower which had began running cold, but from the lack of a release I had been denying myself. After turning off the water, I got into position again. I had never been so hard before and it was a little scary. Instead of panicking, I took a hold of my dick once more and this time I stroke it—alternatively tugging and dragging my palms over the head.

"So good." I whispered. "So—so good!"

This time as my body screamed for release, I listened. I bit into my bottom lip, tightened my fist around my dick and tugged until I couldn't turn back even if I wanted to. Wrapped my other hand around my cock as well and drove my hips into the circles. I pumped my hips harder, faster until the madness took over. I grunted, trying to keep the shout of pleasure in the pit of my stomach.

There was no caring left—no stopping. A pressure built up from the very tips of my toes, shot up my legs and ricochet off my brain. It lit an electricity in me that sizzled off my nipples causing my knees to weaken, threatening to drop me on my face.

By the time white spunk flew through the air, landing on my hand and in the tub, I had completely lost my mind. My body was frozen in a strange arch, my nipples pulsed, and I was completely gone. I slumped to one knee in the tub and bowed my head.

This was different.

Ellie Sargent was doing some crazy strong things to me and I couldn't give in to them. I couldn't manhandle her like I had done before. I needed to get to the bottom of this bullshit with her father and let her go. If not, I knew for sure, I'd betray my family.

—betraying my family would kill me. They'd given me a life and a family when I had none. It was because of them I had a roof over my head, I was able to play music and grew into something my mother could be proud of.

After my parents were killed in a car accident, the rest of the family turned their backs on me. I wasn't sure why and I was too young to even realize something was seriously wrong. The Jonas family took me in, gave me their name and set me on the right path. They were everything to me and I needed to deny my penis and focus on the love they'd showered me with my entire life.

They claimed me and they didn't care I looked different. Malik had always had my back, telling everyone who would listen, I was his baby brother and therefore off limits.

Not once did I ever feel out of place or unwanted. I had brothers who adored me and parents who never once gave up on me.

No, I couldn't touch Ellie again the way I had before.

I turned the water on again and pushed to shaky feet. It was barely lukewarm, but I needed to clean up. By the time I was finished, my exhaustion kicked in and I simply wanted to sleep. But there was so much to do if I wanted to get the temptation out of my life.

OUR INVESTIGATION GROUNDED TO A HALT. Otis Valentina wasn't an easy man to find. There were layers and layers of people to go through and we seriously didn't have time for that. I then decided to take another approach—his sister. Though she was dead, she had to have been buried somewhere. Hopefully, it was somewhere in Montana. I tasked Swede with the job of finding her. I would have used the child, but we had no way of knowing if the child was alive or dead and if Otis didn't like the kid, he wouldn't be registered in any schools.

"Okay, so I found four women who matches his sister's description, with the same name and who has had children in the last ten years." Swede was still tapping away at his keyboard as he spoke. "You're going to need help running all of them down and we don't have the manpower to spare right now. Taz is on assignment."

"Don't worry about it." I told Swede. "I have a few people I trust."

"Okay, good. Listen, how is she doing?" Swede asked.

"As good as one can be after finding out her father was a manwhore who knocked up a gangster's sister while still married to her mother."

Swede groaned. "I have to run. I've sent the information for the women to you. Let me know what you find. Call if you need anything, cool?"

I nodded. "Very."

Swede smirked and his face disappeared off the screen. I was about to head up the stairs to wake Ellie, when a car pulled into the driveway. I picked up my gun from where it sat and shoved it into the back of my pants. Carefully, I made my way to the front and peeked out. My mother's SUV was parked beside my car. She had her keys, so I went back to work. It took her a little while to get to me. I could hear her putting around in the kitchen and figured she'd brought us a small feast. In the meantime, I began going through what Swede had sent over. Mom would get to me sooner or later.

"Did you know Ellie is in love with you?" Mom asked from behind me.

I closed my eyes for a steadying moment then turned to look at her. She stepped forward and kissed my forehead then handed me a piece of sugar cane.

"Hey, baby." She smiled at me.

I immediately bit into the cane, ripped off a section and sucked the juice out. The husk, I dropped in the trash beside my leg. "Where's this coming from?" I asked.

"I spoke with Malik." She explained. "She was jealous of you and Susan. I'm not sure how to feel about this."

"Then stop thinking about it." I sighed. I knew there was something there. Ever since she was falling asleep and muttered how beautiful I looked to her. But I'd ignored it. Then the instant in the office where I'd all but ripped her clothes from her body and she did nothing but gave in to me. But love?

Shit—love was such a strong word. I ran from it for I knew when it came to lovers, love was merely a catalyst to get what they wanted. Those words coming from Ellie would probably kill me.

"You do realize she's a beautiful woman, right?" Mom asked.

"Mom, I know." I sighed. "I can't let my mind go

there with her. I can't think about her in that way. Not after…"

"Forgiveness, baby."

I frowned. "I could have been locked up, life over. Mom, she accused me of—"

Mom rubbed my back. "Yes, but everything worked out. I often think about that time in our lives. And I think, if we didn't have to leave there…"

"No."

"It was a bad time for us, I'll agree with you there." Mom walked to stand in front of me and to frame my face with her tender hands. Her voice and touch were reassuring. "But try not to think of what could have been."

"Does dad know you're here talking to me about forgiving Ellie?"

"Who do you think dropped me here?" She grinned prettily at me.

I should have known. My father would walk on water if it meant my mom would smile. There wasn't another love on the planet like theirs. They truly went through richer and poorer, sickness and health, good times and bad times—and they stood firm like the giant bur oak tree behind their house.

With a soft sigh, I leaned forward and kissed her nose. "I love you, you know that, right?"

"No duh!" She giggled.

"Mom…"

She used her thumb to caress my cheeks. "Don't close yourself away. If you see she's really changed—be open minded. I don't want you to miss out on something that might be good for you because of past slights. We've raised you well. We've raised you to know how to see darkness and light in people. Whatever you choose, your father and I will stand right here to protect you. And whether you rise or fall, we'll still be here."

"Okay, mom."

"So." She released me to look down at the papers on my desk. "Need to run the case by me?"

I laughed. "I think I have a lead. You hungry?"

"I brought over some patties," she said. "And your father made saltfish and okra—your fave—and I brought you some as well…"

"Where's dad?"

"He went to pick up a few things for the house." Mom explained. "We're preparing for the next family dinner."

"I'm sorry I've missed a couple." I told her.

"Look, saving a life is much more important. We know you didn't do it on purpose."

"Why don't I make a couple of phone calls, then you can join me for something to eat?" I asked.

"And Ellie?"

"Upstairs."

"Okay. You work. I'll wake her to get something to eat."

I wasn't sure that was the best idea. Ellie hadn't seen my mother in years. I had already left her alone with Malik and my brother wouldn't tell me what they talked about or if they had a fight. All he said was, Ellie was different somehow. Still, I nodded, and mom patted my shoulder then left me alone.

Without waiting around, I made the first phone call to Grim and assigned him one of the Mariana Valentina on the list. He accepted the task. My next call wasn't to law enforcement, but to a couple of friends in a biker gang. Actually, they weren't really a gang—Christian Alvarez otherwise known as Xman used to be a criminal but his last prison sentence about ten years before flipped a switch in his brain. He ran a restaurant in Butte with his best friend Olivia. We called her Bunny.

They took on two of the Marianas which left me with one who had died about seven years before of a heart attack. I supposed if Grim, Xman and Bunny found nothing, Ellie and I would be taking a trip to the cemetery.

COBRA

GRIM'S lead was a dead end.

Xman and Bunny found out the woman's real name wasn't Mariana Valentina—apparently, she was a stripper and had taken on the name so her parents wouldn't find out she'd blown through tuition and was now trying to make the money back. I looked over at Ellie who was frowning and knew she was as disappointed and angry as I was.

"Our last hope is this woman at the cemetery." I pointed out.

"Right and since people have been taking pot shots at you, you're not going alone." Bunny lifted her beer to her lips. "Xman and I are going to run backup."

"Don't argue with her, you're not going to win." Xman warned.

"We will take all the help we can get." Ellie told them.

With our plans set, my car was flanked by two Harley Davison motorcycle until we were at the cemetery. Xman and Bunny veered off and I knew what they were doing. Still, I parked, and Ellie and I began the search to find the grave. When we finally did, it was a shame. Otis hadn't given her a tombstone. She was buried in a grave with a wooden cross over it and her name scrawled across the center piece of said cross.

I stood back and watched Ellie fall to her knees and began pulling grass from around the site. "I wish I'd brought some flowers or something." She muttered. "How could he kill her and throw her away like this? Who does that?"

I said nothing. I wanted to explain to her that with men like Otis women meant nothing. They were commodities to be traded, demean, hurt as they saw fit. But I kept the words in and glanced around to see if we were alone or if we were being watched by anyone except Xman and Bunny.

"What happened to your child, Mariana?" Ellie whispered.

"We'll look into that," I told her. "Right now, we need to confirm if this is the Mariana we're looking for. Come, let's go talk to someone inside the funeral parlor."

She extended a hand to me and I accepted and helped her to her feet. There was a change in her, something I hadn't really focused on. Malik was right, but what was I supposed to do with all of that.

I messaged Xman and Bunny, letting them know we were on the move.

Inside the parlour was clean and quiet. It smelled like disinfectant and death. Ellie drew closer to my side and tangled her fingers with mine. I understood what she felt in that moment for I was feeling it too.

"Can I help you?" A man asked from behind us.

We turned and I nodded. "I had a few questions regarding the plot with no tombstone just a cross?"

"Our Mariana…" The man said sadly. "Yes, no one claimed her body after it was brought here from her home. We had to bury her ourselves."

"Can I pay for a stone for her?" Ellie asked.

"Are you family?"

"No." I replied. "We're friends of hers from out of town."

"Splendid!" The man cheered. "It's a sad story—I'm sure you know."

"No. We were living abroad. Hadn't really been in touch for some time." I told him. "We heard it was medical?"

The man looked around then back at us. "Rumor has it, she was involved with gangs. The medical examiner said she had a child right before her death. But no one has been able to find the child. I feel for her."

"Yes," Ellie said, her voice cracking. "Truly sad."

"What do we need in order to get her a stone?" I asked.

"This way please." He escorted us to an office.

It took no time at all to make arrangements for Mariana to get a proper stone. In that time the gossipy director gave us a little more information about Mariana. Apparently, her house was locked up and Otis had refused to sell it. It made no sense he'd hang on to it, since from what Samuel, said Otis was the cause of her demise.

"Our next stop has to be that house," I told Xman and Bunny once we congregated at a local diner for some food.

"Can you get Grim to run backup for you?" Xman asked. "Bunny and I are due in Butte for a meeting with our staff that's been a long time coming. If you need us, we can stay."

"Hey, no worries," I said. "Grim can do it. But thanks for heading out here for this."

"No worries." Bunny nodded. "If you need us to come back…"

"You'll be the first call." I promised.

We finished lunch and Bunny and Xman went on their way after hugs and words of encouragement to Ellie. We rented a truck and made our way to the house to check it out. When we arrived, it was precisely as I suspected—there were cars parked in the front yard. While the windows were boarded up, and someone had gone ahead and erected a chain linked fence around the place with one gate. Cameras were sitting above the front windows and the corners of the roof. I suspected they were showing every angle. It would be hard getting inside and almost impossible getting out.

I drove past the house and stopped the truck a little distance away, then killed the engine and waited.

"What are we waiting for?" Ellie asked.

"This is merely a fact-finding mission." I told her. "This entire thing is even worse with that fence. There are also cameras—four from what I gathered during the quick stop."

She nodded and turned her attention back toward the house. "I don't get why they're protecting the place so much. Mariana is dead."

"They're not protecting the house." I explained. "They're using it as a hideout—a sort of headquarters."

"Is nothing sacred?"

"Not to these people." I explained. "Like we heard, he killed his own sister. You get in the way of their money and you're dispensable. Having a vagina is a curse to a man like Otis. No matter if he loves you or not—you cross him and you're replaceable."

She grunted.

"Look, Ellie, about what happened the other day…"

"Don't say you're sorry."

"I shouldn't have done that." I pushed. "You didn't deserve it."

"If I get what I truly deserved I'd be dead."

"Ellie…"

"Do you hear me complaining?" Ellie asked. "I'm only pissed off because you stopped and just left me there."

"You couldn't have enjoyed that…"

Ellie sighed. "Let's not talk about this anymore, okay?"

"I'm curious."

"About what?" Ellie was angry. "The fact that I allowed you to handle me like that. I was too. I'd never been the kind of woman to want a man to hold me down or anything like that. But there has always been something different about you, Tarek. It's something that makes me unable to think and do dumb things. It's the kind of thing that always made me hot with want, even as a teenager. I'm trying to be better."

I glanced at her quickly then back at the house.

Ellie took one of my hands and carried it across to her thigh. Something told me to pull my hand away, but I was curious to see what would happen. She dragged my hand up her thigh, easing her dress up as it went. Slowly, Ellie pushed my hand between her legs then added pressure to the back. The seat of her panty was wet, and I knew what was happening.

Without further prodding, I slipped a finger inside her panty then into her. To my surprise, Ellie was wet and if we could I would have no trouble entering her. She sighed and rolled her hips, taking my finger deeper.

"See?" She whispered. "I only have to think about your hand at my throat and this happens. Please, Tarek?"

"Ellie we can't...not here."

But she wasn't listening. Ellie was holding my hand and grinding down on my fingers and palm. Seeing her like that made my heart leap. She was so sexy, I wanted to give her more than I should in that moment. I wanted to take it all, to see her face and her body fall apart because of the things I yearned to do to her.

Completely distracted by her moans and the movement of her body, I gave in to what she pleaded for. I fingered her, driving them into her hard and fast while rubbing her clit with my thumb. She whispered my name and soon she had a hand over her mouth as her body stiffened.

"Tarek." She whispered.

I withdrew my fingers and massaged her clit as she mewled and slumped into the seat. She closed her eyes and tears tumbled down her cheeks.

"What's the matter?" I asked, softly.

"I want more, Tarek." She confided, meeting my eyes. "I don't deserve it and I know I shouldn't, but that hasn't stopped me from wanting everything."

I pulled her dress back in place and smiled as I reached across to kiss her forehead. "Let's get back to work. We can talk about this later."

Ellie nodded and pulled herself up in the seat. I took my hand back from her and set it in my lap. The entire interior smelled like her—her perfume, her sex.

The beast that had grabbed her before lifted its head and I had to tamper it down by swallowing the lump in my throat.

"Just so you know, Ellie." I began, my eyes on the happening ahead of us at the front gate of the house. "If we weren't working, you wouldn't be able to walk well for days."

"You promise?"

I looked down at the tent at the front of my pants then back up at the cars pulling up to the gate. "Just take my word for it."

We slipped into silence. People went in and out of the house. When it grew dark, we climbed from the truck and headed closer on foot. It was as if every light was on in the house. Base from the music inside echoed through the night with laughter and cheers. From somewhere in the distance a dog barked, probably annoyed by the bullshit these people were calling music. I tested the fence by throwing something at it.

Nothing happened. I tapped it with a finger but realized it wasn't electrical. I could try climbing it but the barbed wire at the top would definitely be an issue. We would have to find another way in.

Once we returned to the truck, I was frowning. "Maybe we should try another way."

"Is there another way?"

"Maybe." I pulled on my seatbelt and started the ignition. "Otis runs a club here in Billings. It's high end, flashy."

"Guestlist kind of thing?" Ellie asked.

"Yes." I checked the mirrors. "I'm thinking Swede can get us on it. Think you can put an outfit together for tomorrow night?"

"I don't have anything remotely appropriate for a flashy club." I told him. "Everything I have is back in Eagle Rocks—at that house."

I sighed. "I know nothing about fashion—male or female—I think we're going to need Maia for this."

Ellie chuckled. "No surprise there."

"What's that supposed to mean?" I asked.

"It means, I think you're better at getting women out of their clothes than getting clothes on them."

I smirked. "There's only one way to find out."

Ellie moaned. "Yes, please."

After weeks of no rain, the sky opened up halfway to my place. I parked the rental beside my car and Ellie was out the door before I even had the ignition off. She stood at the front of the vehicle, lifted her face to the downpour and smiled. I killed the engine and walked to her. Though I meant to ease her into the house, but she reached for the front of my shirt and dragged me into her. Our eyes met and without words, I took her mouth under mine in a lip-bruising kiss. I tangled my fingers in her hair and pulled her hair back.

Ellie looked up at me, her eyes daring me, teasing me. Unable to stop myself, I gripped the front of her wet dress and tugged. The searing sound of material coming a park was silenced by the sound of thunder scraped across the sky. We weren't going to make it into the house.

Picking her up, I carried her to the bed of the truck. I sat her on the edge of the back and shoved her legs apart. I wasn't careful with her clothing—I shredded them with my fingers and discarded the pieces behind me.

As she lay there, naked under the moonlight with rain pelting down, I couldn't understand how she was so sexy. I was jealous of the rain caressing her body, making her arch upward for more. She rested on her back and I spread her legs and bowed forward. I ate at her, swirling my tongue around her clit, sucking at it, listening to her scream for me. She reached for me, but I held her hands down, restraining her while I took my fill from her.

"Tarek, I want to…" She gasped. "Touch you."

But I wasn't ready.

She came for me, hard and rough. She squirted into

my mouth, hot and sweet and I growled. I licked it all up and drove her again to another. Her legs shook as she tried pulling her hips away. But I latched on. The creature in me had tasted her and I wanted to do it again and again until I had my fill.

Ellie managed to wiggle away, and I slipped in the water and fell.

That didn't stop her, Ellie scooted from the truck and climbed on top of me. After peeling my shirt off, Ellie took over. She kissed me roughly while holding my hands to the ground over my head as she used my mouth like I used my tongue between her legs.

I gave her free reign of my body—of moving downward, kissing, biting, licking until she was face to face with my clothed dick. She struggled with my belt then the zipper. Finally, the rain flowed over my freed cock and it throbbed in her hand then her mouth. When I tried sitting up to watch her, she pressed a hand to my chest and shoved me back.

I held the back of her head and eased my dick down her throat. Ellie gagged but didn't pull away. Instead, she dug her nails into my abs and took me deep again.

I had no words. Controlling what my body did for her wasn't anything I could have done. I gave in to her, driving my hips up and into her mouth.

"Shit, Ellie!" I growled.

She sucked on me, fondling my balls, squeezing and rubbing them. When it became too much, she dragged her mouth to my shaft, sliding her tongue up and down along the outside and my eyes rolled to the back of my head.

"I'm gonna come if you don—Ellie!"

She stopped. "Oh, no you don't! Not yet. I'm not ready for you to do that yet."

I panted. Water falling into my face blurring my vision and driving me crazy. I scooped her up and carried her to the truck. I turned her to face away from me and bend her and slid a finger into her.

"Tarek!"

"Shhh." I covered her mouth with my free hand then replaced my finger with my dick. "You wanted this, Ellie." I withdrew and shoved back in. "So, take it. Take it all!"

She squirmed under me. I released her mouth and gripped her hair to use as leverage. She was already pushing back into me, her body hungrily taking me the deepest I'd ever been with anyone. I drove into her, causing the truck to rock back and forth.

"Harder!" Ellie demanded. "Give it to me harder!"

Hearing her pleads was music to my ears. My body reacted to hers by growing harder, stiffer. Her pleads made me lose my mind and I rode her hard in the rain.

But it wasn't enough.

It wasn't enough to take her one way. Soon, I was on my back in the mud again with Ellie over me, riding me to one powerful orgasm. She towered over me like a queen I could barely see. Each time I cleared the water from my eyes, the downpour caused me to close my eyes, grip her hips and crash upward into her falling body.

"Yes!" She cheered. "Just like that!"

I took her breasts in my hands and played her like an

instrument. I twisted and pulled her nipples as hard and gentle as she wanted.

When she melted from my body, I came, cum flying through the air and falling to the wet ground. I trembled and Ellie kissed me until the shaking subsided. Still, I held her head in place as I kissed her roughly. She moaned and gave me her tongue then wrapped her fingers around my cock. Each stroke made my body twitch and I groaned and pulled my mouth away when she squeezed the head.

"Ellie…"

"I love it when you whisper my name like that." She whispered, kissing my nipples.

We then laid on our backs in the front yard, her fully naked and me, partially. I didn't care. I knew we should probably go inside. But I didn't trust my knees to work.

"Damn, Tarek." Ellie whispered. "Is that what I'm missing?"

I said nothing.

ELLIE

I WAS STILL BRUISED by the next day. Having Tarek over me, all powerful, had driven my body into the ground but I wasn't complaining. Every time I thought about the way he was with me, aftershocks from my orgasms raged through me.

I dressed in a pair of jeans and a tank then draped a thin black shawl around my shoulders to hide and discolouration to my body.

Though Tarek hadn't been okay with the idea, Maia talked him into letting us go alone to buy a few outfits for the mission that night.

He watched me with the expression of a puma ready to devour me. I trembled and melted under his stare, knowing he had the capability to turn my entire world into an erupting volcano.

I love knowing he could. I licked my lips and allowed Maia to usher me out the door and to her jeep. As we sped through the streets, the breeze coming in through the window after an all-night rainstorm was refreshing. I closed my eyes and smiled.

"Can I confess something to you, Maia?" I asked after a while.

"Sure."

"For the first time in ever, I'm ashamed of what I've done with my life."

"And what have you done with your life?"

"Nothing." I replied. "Zilch. Diddly-squat."

Maia glanced at me then back at the road. "What do you mean nothing? Education? A career?"

"Nothing." I sighed and turned my gaze back out the window. "I didn't bother with college. I had daddy and daddy had money and I thought that was all I needed. But the thought of Tarek seeing me as a failure hurts more than I thought it would. It's like someone taking a hot knife and plunging into my chest and suddenly, I can't breathe."

"Well, it's not too late to change that." Maia advised. "What are you good at?"

"Nothing."

"Come on. Everyone has that one thing they're good at."

"Not me."

"Seriously, think."

I exhaled loudly and tried doing as she demanded. The truth was, I never thought I needed a hobby. Money talked and because of that I always had what-ever I wanted. "I wasn't even a part of any after school clubs. Can you imagine that? I'm a wasted human being."

"Don't say that." Maia told me. "Okay. It's not too late to pick up a hobby. All you have to do is find something you enjoy doing. Then, you find some focus and do what you want."

"The only thing I can think about is fashion." I admitted. "I love clothes and shoes. People turn that into something worthwhile, right?"

"Every day."

I sighed. "My father managed to lose all the family's money." I told her. "I think that's why he ripped off a drug dealer—to replace it. But he couldn't touch my inheritance because I had become an adult and had control of it."

"And if you don't mind me asking—how much is that?"

"About seventy-five million." I explained.

She whistled.

"It wasn't all his money." I told her. "My grandfather was into oil, so he left a chunk of it to me when I was a kid. My father added to it over the years."

"That's still a lot of money," Maia said.

"I'd give it all up if Tarek would just..." I hung my head.

"Seriously, you should tell him."

"I know but when I was a kid..."

"About that." Maia glanced at me. "What did you do?"

"Accused him of rape."

"Oh shit. That explains why he's pissed off at you enough to light things on fire."

"That's putting it lightly." I frowned. "I saw him with

another girl, and I lost my god-damn mind. It was a stupid as hell thing to do, but I thought it was the best thing I could ever have thought up at that time. Told my father don't press charges just fire Tarek's father. As I gloated, his anger was like a knife, tearing through my flesh and boy was he mad. I'd never seen him like that before and if I'd known better, I would have been scared."

"I'm not going to excuse what you did." Maia told me. "But jealousy makes us do stupid, hurtful things."

"Trust me, I know."

"The good news is, you can always make amends." Maia checked the mirrors and pulled into the mall's parking lot. "Tarek is a good guy. All you have to do is show him you've changed. Show him you're a better person than the kid who almost ruined his life and that will go a long way into helping him see you differently."

"I don't know how much difference that's going to make." I picked up my purse and let myself out the front of the vehicle and closed the door.

We walked side by side toward the entrance, Maia's eyes darting around. Tarek did the same thing when we went into public. I knew what they were doing—trying to spot the danger before it saw us. Once inside, she looked around as if mentally taking pictures of the exits and entrances, staircases and escalators. I did the same. Though I doubt I would remember them all, taking stock of my surroundings had become the norm since my father managed to sell my soul to the devil.

Usually, in the mall, I would wander from store to store. This time, I wasn't there for fun. Instead, I headed straight to a specific store where I could get everything for the night. First, I needed to pick out an outfit that said *I came to slay.* Each outfit I exited in, Maia shook her head.

"Come on, girl!" Maia pouted. "Fashion is your thing, remember? Just think, you want an outfit that will knock Tarek off his feet."

I guffawed. "Sure, yeah. That will happen."

"Don't be so cynical. Try the next one."

I frowned and closed myself into the stall again. This time, I slipped in a black corset that pushed my breasts up to my eyebrows, paired it with a black pencil skirt that clung to my curves and slipped my feet into cherry red, sky-high stilettos. When I stepped out, Maia's eyes widened. "What do you think?" I did a runway twirl.

"That's the outfit." She gave me the thumbs up. "What size shoes do you wear?"

"Eight."

"Perfect. I'll be borrowing those at some point."

I laughed. "Just say the word."

"You do know I'm not joking, right?"

I nodded. "I know. Me either."

We bought the outfit along with the shoes, makeup and a few other things I needed like makeup and nail care. I secretly picked up a bracelet for Maia. We exited the store and Maia instantly drew close to my side. It didn't take a genius to know something was up.

"Keep walking." Maia told me. "He's been watching us since we were trying stuff on."

My heart fluttered inside my chest. I was getting really pissed off with people taking shots at me. I wanted to be able to go to the damn mall and not have it turn into a fucking international incident. Still, I reigned in my anger and followed Maia's instructions. We were almost at the exit when people started shouting. Men were shoving by them. One lady was tossed into a nearby fountain and she screamed loud enough to wake the dead.

Maia grabbed my hand and tugged me through the shocked onlookers until we realized our exit was blocked.

"BPD!" Maia yelled. "Out of the way!"

People scrambled to clear a path for us, but the door was still blocked with men I knew belonged to Otis' gang. Instead of stopping, Maia pulled her gun, aimed and fired. I didn't think I would ever get used to the sound of a discharged weapon. This time, I didn't scream. I tugged my hand from hers and kept running. One man came at Maia and I lashed out with a foot catching him in the cock. His eyes rolled back, and he slumped to the ground. I brought my knee up to his chin as hard as I could and there was a snapping sound as he hit the floor face first.

I had no time to celebrate my take down. Someone grabbed me from behind and I dropped my weight on his arms. Luckily, it worked, and I hit the ground hard. When the man reached for me again, I lifted one hand and poked him in the eyes, rolled away and pushed to my feet. This time, I ran toward Maia as I heard her gun went off again. I looked back to see my pursuer falling to the ground with a gaping hole in his chest.

As I reached Maia, she was on her phone. "Back up!" She said.

I needed no prodding to get through the doors and skidded to a stop outside the entrance as police scars screeched to a halt. Since nine eleven, cops weren't usually far away from major places with large crowds.

Maia exited with her badge hoisted in the air. Immediately, the men fell in line and she began barking instructions. The cops darted into the building and Maia ushered me to her jeep. I climbed in, dropped my bags on the floor and exhaled loudly.

"I'm getting so fucking sick of this shit!" I growled. "All because he couldn't be loyal to the woman he chose —the woman who loved him. He had to stick his cock in every damn dark hole he could find!"

"Calm down."

"Don't tell me to calm down!" I snapped. "I'm not lady Rambo! I'm not used to guns and bullet to the brain!"

"But you handled yourself like a pro in there." Maia told me. "Tarek would be proud."

Hearing that took the bite off my anger. Having Tarek be proud of me rather than anger at me was a good feeling. I exhaled loudly again.

"I don't want to die, Maia." I told her soberly. "I don't want to die."

"No one is dying..." She opened her mouth to say something else, but her phone rang. "Cobra, calm down. I got her. She's good... yeah. I'm extracting her now. Okay, sure."

Maia handed me the phone and I pressed it to my ear. "Tarek?"

"Are you okay?"

"Fine. Maia was a ninja."

Maia laughed.

"We're on our way." I told him.

"We need to end this." Tarek told me. "I'll run you a bath."

"Sounds like heaven." I wanted to ask if he would join me—maybe make love to me in the bath, but I held those questions to myself. I didn't know if he wanted Maia to know what we'd done. I didn't know if he wanted anyone at all to know. For some reason, that worry made me ashamed. "Thank you."

"Ellie?"

"Hmmm?" I bit into my lower lip to keep the tears at bay now burning my eyes.

"What's wrong?"

I sighed. "Nothing. We'll see you soon."

I hung up and set the phone in the holder attached to Maia's dashboard. Once I did, I glanced back to see if we were being followed but we were the only ones on that stretch of road. After a few minutes, my body began shaking.

"Adrenaline crash is a bitch." I muttered.

"Tell me about it." Maia agreed. "Relax. Take deep breaths. The shaking will stop soon."

"You don't seem to be having that issue."

Maia chuckled. "As bad as it sounds, I'm used to being shot at. It kinda comes with the territory. But it's not for everyone, I get that. It's why I've been single for a very long time."

"Men are stupid."

Maia laughed. "I can't disagree with you there. If I was willing to settle, to give up a part of me, I could have been married a long time ago. I almost did. Then I thought...*how happy would I be if I gave up my career for him?*"

"A man who really loves you would never ask you to give up your soul to make himself feel like a man." I told her. "A *real* man would never ask you to give up your soul to make him feel like a man. You made the right decision."

"I know." She pulled into Tarek's driveway and turned off the ignition. "Sometimes when the loneliness becomes too much—I wonder."

"Listen, I've met the most amazing guys in the Protectors—Tarek's friends." I giggled. "I'm pretty sure if I asked, they could point me in the direction of a good one."

Maia laughed. "Absolutely not. Besides, I'm pretty sure they are all with someone."

"It's worth a try." I pointed out. "I mean, if Kujo wasn't with someone—or Swede—lord have mercy."

"Keep it in your panties, Dirty Harriette." Maia giggled. "We need to behave."

"Oh boo—"

The front door opened, and Tarek and Malik stepped out. They stood akimbo, staring at the jeep and I knew our pause in the vehicle had gotten us in trouble.

"Oh, I think we're about to get a spanking." Maia teased while unclipping her seatbelt.

"Oh gawd, I hope so." I muttered.

Maia laughed out loud and pushed her door open.

"Shit, did I say that out loud?" I whispered.

"Yup!"

My cheeks heated.

Inside, Malik found us something to eat while we told Tarek what had happened. Maia hugged me and had to leave to fill out reports of the incident. I walked her to the door and when we stepped outside, I pulled the box from my pocket and extended it to her.

"I can't." She shook her head. "It's too much."

"You don't know what it is," I said. "Please, it would mean the world to me if you took it. Even if you never wear it."

"Ellie…"

"My own friends wouldn't have done what you've done for me." I told her. "Thank you seems so—not enough."

"Ellie, you're friends with Tarek…"

"No, not really."

She chuckled. "You know what I mean."

"Please."

Maia sighed but accepted the box and opened it. "This is lovely. Thank you."

I nodded. "Be careful."

"I will." Maia touched my cheek then climbed into her truck. "You know Tarek is afraid for you?"

"Yeah, because if I die on his watch…"

"Girl, come on, man." Maia leaned out the window. "Take a closer look."

For a moment I said nothing. When her engine went on, I stepped back and wrapped my arms around myself. I headed back inside as she reversed.

Inside, Malik was on the phone. Tarek took my hand and led me into the office. He closed the door and eased me into the hard surface.

"I'm going to ask again." Tarek met my eyes. "Are you okay?"

"A little bruised, but you should see the other guy."

He smiled. "I'm going to run you a bath." He said.

I grabbed his shirt to stop him. "Call me needy but I would like you to kiss me." I hung my head. "I want to feel your hands on me, to hear you breathe in my ear— why am I like this?"

Tarek turned and peeled my fingers from the fabric of his shirt. He used his body to hold me to the wall and pressed his mouth against my ear. I sighed, closed my eyes and waited. His scent was intoxicating—strong, woodsy. He moved his cheek against mine, the day-old stubble grazing my skin, turning me on.

"You're saying you want me, Ellie." He whispered huskily before nipping at my earlobe. "Don't beat around the bush. Say the words."

"I..."

He leaned back and quickly spun me to face the door. I braced both hands on it before his body was back against mine. He reached down to grab my ass in his large palm and squeezed. "Say the words."

I moaned.

He spanked me. "Say. The. Words."

I melted down my own leg and gasped as his hand marked my cheeks for him. "I want you." I conceded. "I want you right now."

"Good girl." Tarek growled while tugging my thong to the side.

He filled me hard and fast from behind. I tried keeping my scream of delight in. I tried being a good girl, to think about how inappropriate this had gotten. But he pulled out only to shoved back in and every word I wanted to throw out died in my throat. I panted and arched back, shoving my ass out for him to take me deeper, harder, faster.

Tarek didn't disappoint. He rode me like I craved and after my first orgasm, he spun me around, covered my mouth with hand and found me again. I met his gaze, not believing how unbelievable wrong yet sexy it was to have him like this.

"Tell me how you want it." He growled. "No, don't look away."

"Tarek..."

"Yes, Ellie?"

"I want it harder." I moaned while digging my fingers into his shoulders. "I want it every way you can give it to me."

He lifted a hand to my throat and held my neck in place so I could watch him. He wanted me to watch him break me apart and my body succumbed to the thought. I slumped into his chest and the motion caused him to slip from my body.

I pushed him backwards toward a chair then slipped

to my knees in front of him. He cradled my neck and I went down on him, trembling, moaning, sucking.

"Ellie."

My only reply was to fondle his balls and pulled him to the back of my throat. I knew Tarek was almost there —every sound he made, every time his body stiffened, every twitch of his mouth. When he tried to push me away, I held onto the arms of the chair and merely pulled him deeper into my mouth until he exploded.

The happiness that caused me was unbelievable. It was dirty and wrong, but I could muster the capacity to feel even a little bit ashamed about it. The momentum of me pulling off him sent me to my ass. All I did was met his eyes, while his spunk slipped down the corners of my mouth.

COBRA

P LANS FOR THE CLUB CHANGED. After Malik left us for the night for an emergency surgery, Ellie darted up the stairs with her shopping to shower and get ready. It took me no time at all to dress, but it seemed to have been taking Ellie a lot longer. As I paced the kitchen, the computer on the island beeped. I looked down just as Swede's face filled the screen. "Christ on a cracker." I muttered. "That is creepy."

Swede smirked. "What's the matter, Snake-man? I'm not cute enough for you?"

"You're an asshole, you know that?"

"I've been told." Swede laughed. "But listen, I have some new information for you. I've been doing some digging into Otis and his group. I found out seven years ago his sister gave birth to a little boy she named Lilo. After she gave birth, Otis killed her."

I held my breath to pressed down my anger. "Go on."

"But the child is still alive, I think."

"How do you know?"

"I found an account he's been using to pay a nanny service. He didn't sign up for the nanny using his name though."

"Then how do you know he's the one using it?"

"The bank account is his," Swede explained. "The person who hired the nanny wasn't Otis."

"Then who?"

"Mariana."

I tilted my head. "Did he get careless?"

"No. I think he believed we wouldn't be looking for any movement on his sister's name." Swede looked down and began typing away. "This might mean we know where the kid is."

"Yup." Swede replied. "I just sent the address to your phone...Damn."

"What?" I asked.

"Turn around."

With an arched brow, I did as Swede suggested. "Damn..." I managed.

Ellie picked at the corners of her fingers as she stood there, looking good enough to eat. I wanted to take her back up the stairs and tear every piece of clothing from her body except the corset. That I wanted to use my teeth on, to watch as her breasts slowly popped from the neck and come free for my mouth.

"Cobra..." Swede's voice was far away. "King?"

I swung to look at him.

"Down boy." Swede teased in a soft voice. "Do this first before you ravish the lady, please?"

Ellie giggled.

"You're an..." I began.

"Asshole." Swede laughed. "Got it."

His face disappeared from the screen and I closed the computer. "You look...wow."

"Thanks." Ellie smiled. "But why do I get the feeling we have some bad news."

"You should sit down."

"Just tell me." She frowned. "I already know it's going to be horrible. Seems to be going around so, um— like a band-aid. Let's do it."

For a moment, I watched her, debating if I should insist on her sitting. But after a second I merely shrugged. "We believe we found your brother." I told her.

"A brother..." Ellie blinked and sat. "I have a brother —is he..."

"He is seven and his name is Lilo." I continued. "We think he's alive and we know where he is."

"Lilo? Where is he? We should go!"

"Wait a minute!" I grabbed her arm to stop her rush for the door. "The first thing you're going to do, is change. You dressed like that is a crazy distraction."

Her cheeks flushed.

"Then, you're going to have a drink with me and in the morning, we drive to Butte and stake out the nanny until she leads us to Lilo."

"Or we could make her tell us."

"*Puedes atrapar más moscas con miel que con vinagre,*" I told her.

"Say what now?"

"You can catch more flies with honey than with vinegar."

"You speaking Spanish…I'm going to change."

I laughed as she all but ran from the room. "Does it turn you on, Ellie?"

"Shut up!"

All I did was laugh harder.

Strange, something had changed between us. Instead of questioning it, I grabbed my gun and let myself out the backdoor. It was time for my nightly check of the perimeter to make sure we were still safe.

My mind went to Ellie and our sleeping together. It was one of the most amazing moments of my life. Her body was perfect—curves in the right places and I lost every bit of me with her. It was easier since my mother had forgiven her. Malik was a little on the fence and my body seemed to have taken her for her impressions she had changed. How much longer could I have really carried the hate? And it meant something she was back in my life—right?

I moved the vehicles into the garage then entered the house through the side door and set the alarms. When I entered the house, Ellie was in the kitchen peering pensively into a pot.

"Hungry again?"

"My body is still coming down from almost getting kidnapped. It burns through food like crazy." She grabbed a plate and shared some rice and chicken.

"People deal with that differently. For Maia, it's scotch."

"That's too rough for my blood." She glanced at me over a shoulder then went back to the food.

While she did that, I poured her a glass of wine and

me a shot of whiskey. We sat together silently, and she stared at me openly.

"What?" I asked.

"I love it when you're not mad at me." She whispered. "I really didn't mean to be such a bitch. And I'm really trying to find some way to make it so that you can look at me like a woman rather than the medusa who almost ruined your life."

I bowed my head then met her gaze again. "It's a way to go. I'm not going to lie. But it's possible."

She smiled. "I'm glad. How have you really been, Tarek?"

"Been okay." I replied. "It was tough there for a little bit until—well, my parents won the lottery."

"Oh!"

"Yeah…Malik and I went to school. We have a little brother…"

"Jesse—I remember. Hopefully he was too young to remember my stupidity."

I smiled. "I've been okay…I joined the military for a while there. Stayed in until I was hurt and realized my body wouldn't be able to keep going at the rate, I wanted it to."

"So, you come home and joined the US Marshals? I don't think you thought that one through."

"How so?"

"It's still going to be hell on your body."

I laughed. "Maybe you're right. But I'm not remotely good at anything else."

"You were an amazing musician."

"You remember that?"

"Yeah, of course." She finished her food and eased the plate away from her. "I remember standing at the side of the stage listening to you belt out Dashboard Confessional. All the girls were watching you."

"They were?"

"Of course!" She sipped from her wine. "They all had eyes for you. They especially wanted you because you were Malik Jonas' kid brother."

"That took a while for people to actually accept. Malik didn't give a damn. He kept right on telling people I was his baby brother."

"He loved you then. He loves you now."

I smiled. "I know."

"Are we going to talk about it?" Ellie asked.

"About what?"

"What happened between us." She told me. "About earlier…"

I leaned back in my seat and leveled my stare on her. "Okay. Let's talk about it."

Ellie turned the entire glass of wine to her head and didn't lower it until the wine was gone. She then closed her eyes and inhaled deeply. When she opened her eyes again, Ellie had herself together.

"I've had a thing for you since high school." Ellie spoke softly, slowly. "Granted, I didn't go about it the right way. I didn't know how to approach you without embarrassing myself and I never meant to hurt you at all. But now here we are, and you've—well, for the lack of a better word, fucked me, and I want it to mean something."

"What exactly do you want it to mean?"

Ellie's shoulders rose and fell. "I'm hoping it means we can at least try being more to each other. I'd like you to ask me out—on a date...or is that pushing my luck?"

I laughed. "It's not pushing your luck." I leaned forward. "Listen, Ellie, I want to believe you've changed. I can't do the games and the bullshit. I want a woman who will want me for what I can bring to the table and love me for me. If you can't do that, or you can't grow to do that, then this will not work. I will give you everything..."

"I don't want everything—I don't want money or materialistic things."

"I didn't mean those either." I explained to her.

"So, we're on the same page."

We talked a little longer and soon crawled into bed. For the first time, we shared a bed together for the night. I pulled her into my arms and kissed her head.

"Sleep."

She sighed and snuggled into my side.

We didn't speak. There was something about the moment we were in that would be tainted if we'd added words. She kissed my bare chest and shifted until her ear was over my heart. Eventually, she dozed off, but I remained awake. Somewhere along the short journey we'd started the day Taz brought her back into my world, my feelings for her had switched.

I'd fought it, tried telling myself she wouldn't change. But mom was right. If she was lying and was the same person as before, then I would be hurt but I would have my family to lean on. If she was changed, I would be missing out on happiness because I refused to walk into whatever were doing with an open mind.

Malik believed I didn't want to settle down and have a family. Of course, I did. Spending the rest of my life alone wasn't a good thing. The fear of finding another woman like Ellie had been terrified me. I didn't want to take the chance.

At some point, I managed to sleep but I was up again first thing the next morning. Ellie was still cuddled into my side, a leg tossed possessively across my thighs. I smiled but my bladder was screaming at me.

I reluctantly climbed out of the bed. After I'd used the bathroom, flushed and washed, I headed downstairs to make coffee. I found Malik in the kitchen, unpacking food.

"I hope you know what you're doing." Malik told me.

I didn't have to ask what he meant. "I have no clue." I admitted. "If it ends bad, I'll show up at your place and you'll have the strong drinks and junk food to cure my broken heart."

Malik turned to look at me but laughed. "I'm serious."

"So am I." I poured myself some coffee. "I can't keep closing myself off."

"But her?"

I shrugged. "I'm sorry. I didn't mean to disappoint you."

"Come off it, Tarek." Malik frowned. "You have never disappointed me. And I don't think you could ever do that."

I kissed the side of his head. "How was your surgery last night?"

"Good—we're waiting now to see if infection kicks in or if she's out of the woods." He stared at me for a moment. "I worry about you, you know that, right?"

I took a couple sips from my coffee then nodded. "Of course, I know that. And I worry about you too—its in the contract."

Malik makes a face. "You've forgiven her?"

"Kind of."

"Kind of?"

"We had the talk last night about how I was feeling about that entire mess." I set the mug down and stoke a sausage from one of the containers. "I told her I wanted to believe she's changed but it's going to take some time. Ellie seems okay with that."

"I'm going to trust your judgement, Cobra. But if she hurts you again—"

"I won't."

We both swung around. Ellie walked into the room, dressed in one of my shirts. I arched a brow.

"It took me a long time to get to this part and I don't want to lose it." Ellie explained. "You don't have to believe me—I'll just spend all my time proving it. My father always said *actions speaks louder than words.*"

Malik seemed satisfied with that. "Come get something to eat. I hear you two have a long drive a head of you."

Ellie nodded and Malik set a plate in front of her so she could grab some food. I watched their interaction and knew my brother was trying. It made things a lot easier.

Sure, the fear she may lose her mind and do something crazy was still at the back of my mind. It wouldn't go away overnight—I was prepared for that. After all, I was already falling for Ellie and to stop now, would break more than I cared to admit.

ELLIE

I̲t̲ ̲s̲e̲e̲m̲e̲d̲ Tarek was also my protector in my dreams as well. In his arms, the nightmares remained at bay, and for the first time in months, I had a good night's sleep. Tarek shifted under my body and I was awake. He kissed my forehead a few times then tapped my nose gently causing me to smile. I stretched like a cat in the sun, but I didn't yawn. The last thing I wanted was for my morning breath to knock him out.

He dropped a kiss to my nose and climbed out of bed as his phone had been ringing.

"Hey Jesse," Tarek said.

He didn't leave the room right away. Instead, he watched me, a slight tent in the front of his pants. I giggled and pointed to the door.

Tarek groaned but left. Though I had wanted to spend a little time with him that morning, I couldn't be needy. His life didn't revolve around me. Instead of complaining, I climbed out of bed, showered and dressed in a pair of shorts and an oversized Montreal

Expo t-shirt. I made my way down the stairs and headed to the coffeemaker. Tarek was still speaking with his youngest brother Jesse, and I didn't want to interrupt.

I figured I could start breakfast, but as I stared into what should be scrambled eggs, I realized I had failed miserably. For a few minutes, I tried saving what I had been cooking. But the more I tried, the worse it looked, and I knew there was no making it right. I grumbled under my breath and stomped my food in irritation.

Tarek peeked over my shoulders at the tail-end of his conversation and laughed. "Not a cook, are we?"

"Bite me."

He nipped my shoulder.

"Hey!" I laughed.

"Why don't we pick something up on the way?" He asked.

"That's probably for the best." I agreed.

Tarek kissed my shoulder and headed for the door. "Let me change and grab my shield and gun."

I shivered at the thought of that badge on his hip. It took some doing to pull myself together and was ready to go by the time he returned. We stopped at a takeout restaurant and picked up something to fill our stomachs.

My main concern, however, was coffee.

Butte was a three-hour ride away. And Floral Park was a place of luxury and white picket fences. It was the kind of neighbourhood I'd want to raise Tarek's kids in. I glanced over to find him smiling at me. It was as if he could read my mind and knew precisely what I had been thinking.

My cheeks flushed and I looked away.

"We can't stake the house out." Tarek's voice was filled with annoyance.

"How comes?"

"Look around." Tarek was staring into the rear-view mirrors. "The truck would stand out like a sore thumb and the people who live here, will know the Nissan doesn't belong. We can't take the chance Otis has people staking out the place and reporting back to him before we have a chance to see what's in that house."

"There's always a downside."

"It's not all bad." Tarek cleared his throat. "We're in luck though—according to Swede, the house across the street is an Air BnB."

"Are you suggesting me rent it?" I asked.

He nodded as he checked the mirrors then pulled back into the street. "That's the best approach right now. We can't barge in there, guns blazing. If Lilo is in there, he could get hurt and we don't want that."

"Agreed."

"So, right now, we rent the place as a vacation home and we keep watch until we can come up with another plan."

"Is this how you usually work?"

"What do you mean?" Tarek asked.

"It just seems to be a lot of hurry up and wait." I told him. "Patience seems to be the big key to being in law enforcement."

I chuckled. "You have no idea."

When we were a distance away from the neighbour-hood, Tarek pulled over. He tapped away at his phone then called Swede for some help. In no time at all, Swede had us book the home under aliases and we were ready to go in using a code the owner had sent to Swede. We stopped at a nearby supermarket to pick up enough groceries to last us a few days. According to Tarek, the less we had to wander around the community and be seen, the better.

I didn't disagree. We had a gangster wanting me dead. I wasn't about to take any chances.

On our way from the grocery store, we stopped at Xman's place. We didn't stay long—it was only for Tarek to pick up a large, black bag. I didn't have to guess what it held—I knew. We hurried back to the house, Tarek parked the truck in the garage and closed the door before we entered the house.

Tarek set up a station in the master bedroom. He stuck a camera to the wall outside the window facing the house across the street. Soon, he had the feed running on his laptop. I did the best I could to be useful. I took over watching when he needed to use the bathroom. When he needed food, I helped with that. Eventually, I feel asleep, sitting on the floor with my head on his thigh.

I wasn't sure how long I was sleeping but something gentle brushing my cheeks woke me. When I lifted my head, Tarek kissed my head.

"I want you to see something." His voice was soft.

I rubbed my eyes and sat up. "What's going on?"

"Look."

I looked to the screen he'd been pointing at. In the right corner was a picture. It was a bit grainy, but I could still make out a little boy with sandy blond hair, sucking on his thumb. "Is that Lilo?"

"I'll have to confirm it for sure, but I think so." Tarek replied.

"What now?"

"Tonight, I'll go over to get a closer look."

"What about me?"

"I'm going to need you as look-out." Tarek told her.

"Maybe you should get Xman or Bunny." I trembled. "I don't know if I'm the best person to do this. I don't want you to get hurt. It would kill me. Please kiss—"

Tarek kissed me. He kissed me until I lost my mind and melted into his chest. As I returned his kiss, Tarek lifted his mouth.

"You're panicking, Ellie. I need you to breathe for me."

"It'll be okay." Tarek told me. "You'll see."

We watched the screen for a while, and just before nightfall, Tarek hauled himself to his full height and headed on over. I held onto the small radio he'd given me to warn him should someone showed up. As long as I could see Tarek, everything was fine. When I couldn't see him, I almost lost my mind. My heart throbbed inside me so fast, I winced.

"Please, Tarek." I whispered repeatedly. "Please."

But my silent plea wasn't answered. Something wasn't sitting right, and I hated it. I leaned forward, staring at the screen. "Please..."

Still nothing.

An eternity later, a loud bang pierced the air.

"Tarek!" I screamed.

All I had back was silence.

I lifted the radio to my lips. "Tarek!" I called. "Answer me! Tarek, please baby. I need you to—"

"I'm okay." Tarek grunted. "Stay put."

How did he expect me to stay where I was knowing there was a possibility he was hurt? He didn't sound okay—I knew he wasn't okay.

"Tarek? Talk to me. Please don't stop talking to me."

"We're coming."

"We?"

"I promise." He was breathy.

A moment later, Tarek made an appearance at the side of the house then hobbled across the street. I dropped the radio and rushed to him. He held a child securely in his arms and I locked the door then followed him into the kitchen. He set the little boy on the island.

"Call Xman." Tarek spoke through gritted teeth while handing me his phone. "Give him the address."

While I did as he asked, I watched the way Tarek interacted with the kid. Lilo was filthy with a black eye and matted hair. It was as though he hadn't bathed in forever and someone had taken to beating on him.

It broke my heart and made me angry.

He didn't seem as if he'd eaten in a while either. Though Tarek tried speaking with him in English and Spanish, Lilo said nothing, but when he offered him a donut, Lilo grabbed it and all but shoved it all in his mouth at once.

Tarek was pale and it seemed as though he was

having issues breathing. There was a cut over his left eye and a large dark spot was growing on the front of his shirt at his right side. I arched a brow and after finishing my conversation with Xman, I hung up and set the phone on the island.

"Let me see your side." I told him.

"What did Xman say?" Tarek asked.

"He's coming and bringing the van." I told him while lifting the edge of his shirt. "You're hurt."

"I'm fine, I swear."

"You're not fine." I snapped. "Sit down and let me take a look."

He exhaled. "There's a first aid kit in the bag upstairs."

I took off up the stairs to find it. I grabbed towels from the bathroom on my way back. In the kitchen, we set a large platter of fruit in front of Lilo and I escorted Tarek into the living room. Lilo looked as if he'd been through enough as it was, I didn't want him to see me patching Tarek up too.

He talked me into how to stop the blood, then stitches. Though the sight of blood was unnerving, I couldn't pass out. Tarek was depending on me to make him better and I refused to let him down.

He winced with each stitch to go in because there was nothing to numb the pain. Still, I worked as quickly as I could then wrapped him up. When I was finished, Tarek gripped me at the back of the neck and kissed me deeply. I wish that kiss would help him with the pain—I wish it would magically heal him. I gave him my mouth, allowing him to take what he needed.

I sighed.

"Thank you." Tarek whispered.

I managed a small smile and a nod then rose to clean up the mess. Tarek gritted his teeth while pushing his arms into a shirt. By then, Lilo had gone through almost the entire fruit platter.

"What were they doing with him?" I whispered. "He's starving. And they hurt him…"

"We won't know unless…" Tarek turned his attention to the headlights shining into the house through the glass at the top of the front door. After grabbing his gun from the bag, he held it under the island while speaking in rapid Spanish to Lilo.

The little boy nodded and reached for me. Happily, I picked him up and cuddled him into my chest. Tarek walked up to the front window and peered out. He shoved the gun into the back of his pants and opened the door. Xman and Bunny entered, closed the door and the next little while was a flurry of activities. Xman grabbed the black bag and darted up the stairs while Bunny led me out the door with Lilo. I set Lilo in the mini van and strapped him in with the seatbelt. When I backed up, Lilo panicked and reached for me.

"I'm not leaving," Tarek said. "Trust me on this."

I climbed in to sit beside him just as Xman hurried out the door with the bag and tossed it into the back of the van.

"Xman is going to drive with me in the truck." Tarek turned to Bunny. "You going to be okay?"

"You know I got this." Bunny smirked.

"Meet at Backwater?" Xman asked.

They all agreed and soon we were on the road.

Soon, we were pulling into the front yard of a large house—a mansion. They parked in a massive building that reminded me of a hanger for a plane and the doors were pulled shut with a loud clang. Xman and Bunny led us down some steps, through a well-lit tunnel then up again into the main house.

Bunny showed me where one of the showers were and helped me setting up a bath for Lilo. I also borrowed some shavers from Xman and while Lilo splashed around in the tub, I shaved his head to get rid of the matted hair and searched for bugs. Luckily, I found none.

While the others talked, I sat on the edge of the tub, watching over this kid who was now the only family I had left. He was the splitting image of my father, only he had dark eyes—I assumed those came from his mother.

He was a beautiful boy, but I knew he must have been through hell.

"Um—*mi nombre es Ellie. Estoy—su hermana.*" My Spanish wasn't as fluent as it could have been. I had paid very little attention in school. The truth was I didn't see the point. But now as I looked into the eyes of a scared little boy, I needed to find a way to speak to him—to comfort him.

"*Mi hermana?*" He asked. "*Verdad?*"

"Yes."

I sat on the floor and helped him bathe, then rinsed his body. I wrapped him in a towel then washed his clothes in the soapy water. For the moment it was all we had for him until I could get a chance to pick up a few things. I held his hand and led him down to the kitchen and found pancake mix.

Those, I didn't wind up burning.

It gave me great pleasure showing my little brother how to smother his pancakes in butter then maple syrup. The first bite made his face lit up.

I was determined to do right by him. My father wouldn't have stepped up for this kid. I wouldn't let him down—ever.

"Ellie?" Tarek's voice was soft.

I looked away from Lilo for a second. "Hmm?"

"Is he eating?"

I nodded. "And he knows I'm his sister."

"Hey, buddy." Tarek greeted Lilo. "Hermana?"

Lilo pointed to me and my heart soared so high.

Once he'd finished eating, Bunny showed me where he would be sleeping, and I brought him up to bed. I sat with him until he fell asleep then pulled the blankets up to his shoulder. I didn't want to leave him but that was probably the first good sleep he would have had in a while. I asked for Bunny's dryer and tossed Lilo's clothes in.

The house grew quiet after Bunny and Xmas went to bed. I helped Tarek clean up, then checked his wound. It hadn't started bleeding again, but I cleaned it up a little better with antiseptic wash and wrapped it up again. Tarek watched me the entire time and when I was finished, he kissed me again.

"I want to touch you so bad." He told me. "But I'll have to wait."

I smiled. "You're hurt, Tarek. And you must be tired."

"Yes, to both." He sighed and drew me against his good side. "Come here."

I settled against his side, wondering what was next. But for that moment, I'd enjoy the little peace I'd found with him. Then, when he was better, we would rage against the world.

I like that plan.

Otis was going to get what's coming to him—I promise.

COBRA

SLEEP DIDN'T COME the entire night. Aside from Ellie fast asleep beside me, my mind kept floating back to the conditions I'd found Lilo in. The exterior of the house was something out of a movie. The gorgeous mansion with a white picket fence running along the front and a cute little gate. With a pristinely cut lawn and manicured hedges to one side, everyone would believe the home was perfect.

I'd roamed along the outside, being careful of cameras and booby-traps, then let myself in through an open window on the basement level. From somewhere in the house a television had been playing, and I figured as long as it was going, I was more or less safe to wander around.

When I found Lilo, my heart broke and anger pulsed through me. He had been living in a room with feces on the wall, a large pot of urine in a corner and it seemed as though he hadn't been fed regularly. I allowed myself to be distracted, to believe he was pressing himself into the wall away from me because I was a stranger to him.

I later found that to be untrue as stainless steel slid into my skin. I slipped to my knee, trying to move away from the biting pain but it wouldn't stop. I knew if I didn't disarm the person, they'd shove it in deeper and twist.

With nothing else to do, I pulled my gun and placed a bullet up through her chin, exploding out the top of her head. As she fell, I pulled her hand from the knife but didn't remove it until she was lying still on the ground, a gaping hole where her skull used to be. I turned from Lilo, gritted my teeth and yanked the knife out.

The hurt caused me to fall forward on one hand while the other held my side, trying to slow the bleeding.

I was then able to get Lilo, but it was a pain and a half lifting him with one hand while slowing the blood loss with the other. It wasn't until we were eating much later that Ellie asked for her father. He wasn't in the house. But I had Maia send the cops and forensics in. If Jeffery even breathed in the house—they would find it.

I wanted to find out about the nanny service Otis had hired. A large part of me knew the company would be fraudulent.

They'd probably already closed shop.

I exhaled as much as the wound would allow and climbed out of Ellie's arms. It was getting harder and harder to leave her. While she slept, I ventured into the bathroom to check the cut. It didn't seem as though it was infected—yet—and Ellie had done a great job stitching me up. Malik was going to want to see it since he's my brother and a doctor.

After using the facilities, I washed my hands and face then found one of the shirts Xman had supplied me with. I slipped into it and while buttoning it up, I entered the bedroom and kissed Ellie's forehead.

She'd been so scared. Though I was in pain, I could hear the sheer terror as she screamed my name into the chip.

I checked on Lilo who was sitting up in bed watching the door. He scrambled off and underneath it when I stepped through the door. "Lilo?" I gripped my side and knelt in front of it to look under. "Friend—remember?" I asked in Spanish. "It's me, Tarek."

For a silent moment, Lilo didn't move. When he looked around and saw me, he rushed out and into my arms. I grunted and fell to my ass on the floor. Though my side hurt like hell, I held onto him. He was in a delicate spot in that moment where he needed to know I wasn't going to hurt him—I wasn't going to let anyone hurt him.

For an eternity, he clung to my neck, shaking. I wanted to kill Otis then, to put him through the same hell he'd dropped on this child's head. I wanted to starve him, give him a black eye then torture him until every shift in light terrified him so badly, he dove under beds to escape. I wanted to twist him and bend him until he begged me for death.

"Friend." Lilo whispered.

"Yes." My voice cracked. "*Amigo.*"

I somehow managed to pry his arms from around my neck and helped him with washing up and getting dressed in his clothes Ellie had washed the night before. I then brought him into the kitchen to find Bunny was gone and Xman making breakfast.

Once Lilo was set in the living room, watching cartoons and eating, I wandered into the kitchen and pushed onto a stool.

"We should take you back to Billings so your brother can take a look at that wound." Xman told me without looking up from what he was doing.

"I know. But after we get Lilo somewhere safe first."

Xman didn't argue. Instead he placed a loaded plate in front of me. My phone went off and I checked the face—Malik. Someone must have told him I was hurt. I didn't answer and he hung up and called again.

"Are you going to get that?" Xman asked.

"It's Malik—I'm kinda not up for a lecture yet."

"Brother, you can't ignore him forever."

"I know." I groaned. "Where's Bunny?" I shoved some homemade hash brown into my mouth.

"There's a kid in the house." He grinned. "Where do you think she is?"

"Oh gawd!" I groaned. "I hope she doesn't go overboard with the shopping."

"Have you met Bunny?"

She was definitely going to go overboard.

A few hours later, and with an escort from Xman's bikers, Ellie and I set out with Lilo back to Billings. Halfway into the journey, Taz, Reaper and Molly took over the protection. Finding a safe place for Lilo hadn't been hard. Maverick "Reaper" Forge and his fiancé Nova "Star" Shuman agreed to take Lilo in until we could figure things out about Jeffrey and Ellie.

Ellie and I sat on the floor and explained to Lilo we had to leave him. He cried and held onto me until we promised we'd come back for him. We then introduced him to Reaper and Star. Though Lilo was young, the little boy looked up at Star and pressed his cheek into my shoulder while pointing at her.

"Pretty." Lilo told her.

The adults laughed but Lilo was merely embarrassed. With that, the ice was broken and Lilo climbed across into Star's arms.

"I think I'm going to need a shotgun." Ellie teased.

"As long as he knows Star is my girl." Reaper winked.

Ellie crinkled her nose at him, and we laughed again.

We left the house and the first stop was Malik's place. He'd been calling on and off for the better part of the day. When I pulled into his driveway, I turned off the ignition and slumped back into the seat. Ellie reached over and squeezed my hand.

"You okay?" Ellie asked.

"No." I glanced at her then back at Malik's front door. "My brother can be a bit—protective."

"Yes. He loves you—remember?"

I chuckled. "I know." Eventually, I undid my seatbelt and I let us into the house. "M.J?"

There wasn't an answer, so I walked over to the steps and looked up. "M.J?"

Malik hurried down the stairs and framed my face.

He arched a brow, while lifting one eyelid then another. "Grim told me you were hurt."

"Calm down. I'm okay." I told him. "You should see the other girl."

Malik didn't get the joke. Instead he hurried off and soon returned with his medical kit. He brought me into the kitchen, sat in a chair and pulled me close. When he was settled, he lifted my shirt and carefully removed the wrapping Ellie had added. The cool air on my damaged skin was perfection. I turned my head away and groaned.

"Okay." Malik used a finger to press around the wound.

I hissed.

"It's not infected." Malik told us thoughtfully. "There's going to be a scar, but it's better than what it could have been."

"I remember when I was twelve," I said, trying to take my mind off the rawness of the wound. "I fell and the school nurse thought I was faking the pain, so I didn't have to go to classes."

"Seriously?" Ellie asked.

"Oh yes. Because the fact there was a bulge in my arm didn't tell her anything." I glanced down at Malik using a tweezer to test the stitches. "Everyone believed her but Malik—Malik was insistent they took me to the hospital, or he'd call my mother. And trust me, they didn't want Malik to tell mom and explain to her they refused to take me to see a doctor. Malik, you knew it was broken."

"Well, in all fairness, the nurse was an idiot." Malik

muttered as he lathered the wound with anti-septic foam.

I smiled. "All I'm saying is, you've always taken care of me and I don't think I've ever really told you how much I appreciate it."

"Of course, I take care of you." Malik stopped working to look up at me. "You're my brother."

It was that simple for him.

Malik finished with the wound and removed his gloves. He dumped it into the bag with the soiled cotton balls and tied the mouth of it to be destroyed at the hospital.

"It's only a matter of time before Otis comes knocking." I pulled on a shirt, my teeth gritted. "We don't want him anywhere near Lilo or my family. We're going to have to bring the fight to him."

"I hate that plan." Both Malik and Ellie chorused.

"Me too." I kissed Malik's head in a way of saying thanks. "But with me hurt, we couldn't have stuck around Butte to see if he would come back to check out the scene. Now the house is crawling with cops and forensics, he's not going to go anywhere near it. He's not going to risk capture."

"True." Malik pulled a bottle of juice from the fridge. "I hate to say it, but there's a reason that boy isn't dead."

"I agree." I glanced over to Ellie. "Why keep Lilo alive if everyone else who knows of his existence is dead?"

"Maybe they're using him as bait?" Ellie asked.

Malik nodded. "I was thinking that too, Ellie. Maybe they're using him to try and get Jeffrey to talk."

"If that's the case…" I glanced over at Ellie again and

she looked as if her world had just imploded. "What's the matter?"

"If that's the case, these people have no reason to keep my father alive." Ellie exhaled. "I mean, they have no leverage."

"Not necessarily." I walked over to her. "That's if he knows we have Lilo. There's no reason they would tell him. As long as he doesn't know, Otis and his assholes have something to hold over him."

Still, I grabbed my phone. "Swede, I need a solid."

"Name it." Swede told me.

"I need a list of all the properties Otis Valentina has access to or owns." I told him. "And I need it like two years ago."

Swede made an irritated sound in his throat. "Do you have any idea how long that list will be? Otis has money and he cleans it all through real estate trans-actions."

I rubbed my eyes. "Send it anyways. We'll have to narrow it down somehow."

"On it's way." Swede advised me. "What's changed?"

I took some time to explain it all to him. "So, I need everything you have, okay?"

"Roger. When you figure out what you're up to, I'll send a few hands your way." Swede cleared his throat. "You might need the help."

"Thanks." I hung up and faced Ellie and Malik. "The list is coming through now. I'm going to need some help making it shorter."

"Okay." Ellie dragged her palms up and down her thighs. "Let's do it."

True to his word, Swede sent a massive list. Otis seemed to be in the flip business. He'd buy homes, fix them up with help from his boys then turned around and sold them for a profit. I focused on properties he'd hold on to. But the list was still too long. I growled.

"We're going to need more help." Malik said.

I was already making the first call to get Xman and his crew to check out the locations in Butte. Later, I roped Montana in to hit places in Eagle Rocks with help from Bear and Molly.

No luck. I crossed them all off and focused on the two remaining.

"Then there were two." Ellie muttered.

"Only one seemed plausible though." Malik pointed to the addresses. "This one is an open lot. I know because the hospital wants to buy it, but the city is throwing all sort of roadblocks. They want to sell it to a development company."

"If that's true," Ellie said, crossing off the lot. "There's one."

I called Grim.

"I have Maia with me." Grim told us. "What's going on?"

"I'm going to need backup." I told them already checking my gun. "Grim, I need you to meet us at the address I'm about to send you. Maia, can you head on over to my parent's place?"

"On my way," Maia said. "Watch your back, got it?"

I promised I would and after Maia left, I forwarded the address then turned to Malik. "Pick Jesse up on your way over. I'm going to send Taz your way too."

Malik hugged me tightly. "Be careful, please?"

I nodded.

"No, Cobra…say it."

"I promise, I'll be careful." I told him.

Malik hugged me again and was on the phone with Jesse as he rushed out the door. I led Ellie out the door and climbed into the front seat of the Truck and started the engine. She reached across and rested her palm to my thigh.

"I'm sorry I haven't been—well, you know?" Ellie told me. "Up for intimacy. I've been so tired, and you're hurt…"

"Ellie?"

"Hmmm?"

"It's okay. When this is all over, we'll revaluate and go from there." I lifted her hand to my lips and kissed her wrist. "I understand there is nothing sexy about what we're doing right now. You don't have to apologise."

"I thought you would want—you know?"

"And I do. But I understand that has to take a back-seat to everything else right now."

"I'm sorry—this is all my fault."

"Breathe…" I whispered, leaning in to kiss her neck. "Easy."

When we found her father, it would all be over. I knew Jeffrey would put his foot down and though Ellie will want to stand up for me, she will crumble. With her mother gone, Jeffrey would be all she had left, and I was pretty sure if I saved the man's life, Jeffrey will still want me dead.

I checked my mirrors and switched lanes as I sped toward the address. About a block away from our destination, I pulled over behind Grim's truck. My friend climbed out, hurried over and climbed into the backseat of mine. He reached over to tap Ellie on the shoulder in greeting then cleared his throat.

"There's movement inside." He reported. "Nothing's parked out front. I'm guessing they're hiding them in the garage."

"Makes sense." I looked in the direction of the house. "By now, I'm pretty sure it's reached Otis we've been knocking down his doors."

"Well, Maia was saying he might make a run for the airport or a private plane." Grim told us.

"I can see that." Ellie spoke up. "What's the plan now?"

"The plan?" I turned to look over at her. "We go in and try finding your father."

ELLIE

LOVER TAREK WAS STARKLY different than soldier or even US Marshal Tarek. The latter two terrified me. The look in his eyes made me want to hide, even as he did something to his gun and slammed the butt of it into his palm. The weapon clicked and he shoved it into his holster.

"Okay." Tarek said. "Ellie—you should come with us. If your father is in there, he won't want to see me."

I knew Grim wanted to ask me questions, but he climbed out of the backseat. We inched closer to the house and my heart wanted to jump out of my chest. Still, I walked between Grim and Tarek.

Entering the property wasn't easy. I could see the beast raging through Tarek's body. I chewed on the inside of my cheeks as he stopped suddenly causing me to crash into his back. He didn't even look back— Instead, he peeked around the corner quickly then drew back to motioned to Grim. To my surprise, Grim merely nodded and took off toward the other side of the building.

I didn't like that—I didn't want him out of my sight. We had to bring him home. Him leaving meant he could get hurt—Grim could get hurt and then Tarek and Maia would have another reason to hate me.

My heart raced harder, louder and I swallowed the lump in my throat, trying to stop it. Tarek pulled his gun as he seemed to be counting down inside his head. Tarek took a good look at me, peered around the corner then drew in once more.

"Shit." He swore. "Stay here."

All I wanted to do was cling to him. I didn't want him to leave me there. Still, I mustered up enough courage to lift my chin and met his eyes. Tarek inhaled, lifted his gun and stepped around the corner. He fired once then twice, and the air erupted in a boom that threatened to drive me mad. I fought the urge to cover my ears. Tarek motioned for me to go with him.

It was freaky stepping over dead bodies. I wanted to throw up but now wasn't the time to be a coward. As I moved to step over one body, someone grabbed my foot. The fear curled my insides as my heart threatened to leap from my chest. Panicking, I turned and dropped the heel of my free leg into the man's face.

He grunted.

Tarek went Rambo and stepped on his arm while aiming the gun at the man's face. "Let—go."

The man's hand slipped from my ankle and I moved to stand behind Tarek. The roar of Tarek's gun told me the man was dead, and I couldn't even cry. I didn't like people dying around me, but I get it—it was either him or us and I chose us.

I didn't look back.

The sound of another gun went off and was answered by one more. "Grim…"

"He'll be okay." Tarek said as he drew me in through a back door.

I followed him, daze while trying to remain strong. We went through one room after another. Men with guns popped out of dark corners and after a while I felt safe. Tarek was like a dump truck, out of control and careening down a hill. From somewhere else in the structure we could hear Grim going through as well.

When we finally met up, there was one room left. I stood to the side and watched as Tarek and Grim entered the dimly lit space like superheroes. When they called me, I stepped in to find my father tied to a chair with a soft beeping sound echoing in the silence. I mean to run to him but Grim caught my arm to hold me back.

Tarek put his gun away and approached my father. My dad didn't look so good. His eyes were swollen close, his lips were battered and bruised. The beeping continued but I wasn't paying it any attention. I wanted to check on my dad, to feel his pulse.

"What's wrong?" I asked. "Is he dead?"

Tarek reached for my father's neck and shook his head. "He has a pulse."

"So, what's the problem?" I pushed.

Tarek didn't answer. Instead, he walked behind my father and his face fell.

"What?" I looked up at Grim who merely shook his head. "Tarek?"

Instead of answering, Tarek pulled out his phone and lifted it to his ear. "Taz, we have a problem."

I slipped from Grim's arms and ran over to where Tarek was standing. When I looked down, it didn't take a genius to know what was going on. Someone had strapped a bomb to my father's back.

"This is bullshit!" I stomped my foot with tears streaming down my face. "I get him back and now this?"

"Reaper." Tarek hunched down. "I'm going to put video on so you can see what I'm looking at."

Grim took my shoulder and pulled me toward the door. I screamed for Tarek. I didn't want to leave.

"Grim, leave her." Tarek called.

He let me go but I didn't go anywhere. I figured it was the compromise so neither of them worried about me too. Still, she couldn't stop freaking out inside. I bit off my nails, chewed the inside of my cheeks until they were raw and picked at the corners of my fingers until I was sure they bled.

Footsteps outside the room caught our attention and we all looked toward the door.

"Tarek?" I asked.

"Grim…" Tarek called.

"On it."

Grim headed off again and Tarek motioned for me to come to him. He quickly showed me how to use his gun and though I didn't want to, I had no choice. The man I loved, and my father were in trouble. If I had to take down an asshole to protect them, so be it.

"Anyone who comes through that door, that's not Grim or one of the protectors—you point and you fire. Got it?" Tarek met my eyes.

I swallowed and nodded, my hands shaking.

"I'll make this up to you, Ellie." Tarek's voice was steady as he went back to what he was doing with Reaper. "I promise."

I held onto that promise and lifted the gun to the door, trying to block out the sound of gunfire outside and the beep behind me. Footsteps, screaming was chaotic.

"Come on, Grim." I whispered. "Please."

"Reaper, why are the numbers counting down faster?" Tarek asked.

"Reach behind the silver line and snip the cord you find there." Reaper told him.

I didn't hear anything else happening behind me for in that moment, someone, not Grim, barged through the door. Unable to look, I aimed, closed my eyes and squeezed the trigger. The roar was deafening as the force from the gun shoved me backward. Someone groaned and I opened one eye to see what was happening. The man was on the floor. I'd clocked him dead in the chest.

My entire body was shaking but I had to hold on. Tarek wasn't finished—he needed more time.

"Got him!" Tarek called from behind me.

I took a chance and glanced back to see him wrapping one of my father's arm around his own shoulder and pushing up. My father rested heavily into Tarek's side and without being told, I shuffled forward, gun leading me out the door.

The silence terrified me. It was better when people were fighting because I could tell where everyone was. Now, with the quiet, I worried about Grim. But he joined us in the living room, and we tumbled out the door.

A loud bang echoed through the air and a burst of fire tore through my shoulder.

"Grim!" Tarek shouted.

"I got her!" Grim replied before another explosion of noise.

"I'm okay…" I managed. "Get my dad."

But Grim didn't let me go. He took the gun from my hand and scooped me into his arms. My shoulder hurt like hell and it was becoming an issue keeping my eyes opened.

"I need you to keep your eyes open," Grim said. "Talk to me—tell me the first thing you want to do with your dad when he's healed."

"I…I can't." I curled into his arms. "It hurts…"

"I know, beauty." Grim replied. "But if you die on me, Cobra's gonna kick my ass."

I managed to chuckle then groaned.

"We're going to take care of you, Ellie." Grim promised. "You hold on."

It wasn't easy. I tried my best to focus on Grim, his flawless dark skin, big brown eyes and flat nose that made him absolutely one of the most handsome men I'd ever seen—my eyes closed.

"Ellie?" Tarek called. "Keep your eyes open."

I did as he said because I wanted him to be happy. But my body didn't seem to be interested. I gripped the front of Grim's shirt.

"I'm going to have to press on the wound," Grim said. "It's going to hurt but we need to stop the bleeding."

I nodded.

"Ready?"

"Not really, but…"

Grim removed his shirt, bundled it up and pressed it into my shoulder. I gritted my teeth and swallowed the scream I knew had built up from deep inside my soul. I couldn't hold it anymore. I closed my eyes and the darkness came.

It was strange slipping from light to dark, wake to unconscious. The noise of a siren swarmed in on me at one point but, I couldn't be sure. Something soft dropped against my cheek, then my forehead, then my nose. I fought to open my eyes and looked up into the most beautiful green eyes I'd ever seen. I managed a smile.

"Tarek…"

"I'm here." He framed my face and kissed me. "I'm so sorry. I should have kept you safe."

"Stop." I sighed. "I'm so tired—stop it. You were saving my father. You didn't do anything wrong."

"You scared me."

"I'm sorry." I accepted his kiss. "But I'm okay —right?"

"You're great." He leaned back. "The doctors only want to make sure you don't get infected."

"And my dad?"

Tarek released me and sat in one of the chairs beside my bed. He'd withdrawn from me with that one question. I tried sitting up but only managed to flop to the bed. It was probably the medication. I closed my eyes. "Tarek..."

"He's alive." Tarek told me. "But he doesn't want me anywhere near you."

"He doesn't get to make that decision!" I snapped. "After what you've done for him?"

"Ellie—I'm a cop." His voice cracked. "I knew your father wouldn't have been impressed seeing my face. Even though he knows I hadn't done anything wrong."

"Um...I haven't told him."

"I'm going to go." Tarek rose.

"Tarek! Please!"

"Please?" He snapped. "You're saying please? Ellie, you made me fall in love with you and your father still thinks I've violated you in the worse possible way! Do you understand how much that hurts?"

"I get it."

"Do you? Do you really?" He asked. "Because after all these years, your father still thinks I'm an asshole and that would usually not bother me. But a rapist—I can't stay here."

"What's with the yelling?" Maia asked, stepping through the door. "We're going to get thrown out of here."

"They don't have to." Tarek walked out the door.

My heart shattered.

"What in the hell is the matter with the two of you?"

Maia asked. "I thought you had gotten over that whole past thing."

"I haven't told my father I lied." I admitted and tried rolling over. I only managed to roll onto my wound causing me to cry out.

Maia set me back on my back. "Why haven't you told your father?"

"It just got easier not to as the years passed." I admitted. "I never thought I'd ever see him again. Then my father fucked up and here he comes, and I looked at him and…"

I sobbed harder.

"Ellie…" Maia's voice cracked.

"He said he fell in love with me." I cried then. "And once again I managed to stab him in the heart like an idiot."

"You can fix this."

"Maia, I don't think you understand." I sniffled. "No amount of confession to my father will fix this."

"But it's a good place to start." Maia told me. "Right now, get some rest. We can figure out your heart problems later."

I sighed, rolled to my good side and just cried.

COBRA

LEAVING Ellie at the hospital hadn't been easy. I wanted her, needed to feel her against me. But my father always told me never to put my heart ahead of good judgment. I didn't expect Jeffrey to thank me for saving his life. Being a cop in general was a thankless job. But the way he reacted one would think I had tried gutting him like a fish.

I frowned and left my desk to pour myself another mug of bad coffee. When I sat again, I sipped, winced at how bad the stuff was then set the mug beside my monitor. There was too much information to get through on Otis Valentina.

Though my captain wasn't impressed with me coming back without actually resting, he gave in.

"If you can get Otis Valentina off our streets, I'm going to let you run with it." The captain said. "Just don't drop anymore bodies, please?"

"Yeah—I can't promise you that."

The captain had groaned and wandered off toward

his office muttering that *young cops were going to lead him to drink.*

I went through a list of the properties we'd hit. We'd round up a few thugs—none of them would talk. Strange, these men were loyal to a man who would let them rot in prison or die. How could anyone with half a brain, be loyal to a man who would hang them out to dry?

One day melted into two, then three and I wasn't getting any closer to finding Otis. Ellie called daily, but I had yet to pick up, return her calls or listen to the messages she left on my voice-mail. My heart couldn't handle the betrayal that seemed to dig into my chest every moment I thought of her or saw her name flashed on my phone.

"You going to get that?" Taz asked as we sat around having dinner.

"No." I muttered.

"Trouble with Ellie?" Hannah wanted to know. "Need a woman's P.O.V?"

Taz choked. "Say no."

"Hey, I'm good at this." Hannah pouted prettily. "I listen to my clients all the time."

"Not the same thing, sweetie." Taz kissed her pout, then began clearing the table.

"Of course, it is." She insisted.

"You don't have to do that." I told him, rising and taking the plates from his hands. "I need to stand anyway."

"So, can I help?" Hannah asked.

"I don't think anyone can help." I stacked the plates into the sink.

Taz went off to answer a call and Hannah and I continued filling the dishwasher. I explained the entire thing to her and in the end she whistled.

"Yeah," I said.

"Well, I'm not going to make any excuses for her." Hannah sighed. "But maybe she is telling the truth and after you were gone, she didn't see the point. It's probably the coward's way out—easier to just move on."

"It hurts, Hannah." I admitted. "It hurts knowing I allowed myself to fall for her and I still have this blemish over my head."

"Did she say why she did it?"

"She said she was jealous of me with another girl—if she couldn't have me no one else could." I frowned. "I should be flattered she wanted me so much to do something stupid. And sure, no harm, no foul. But one person thinking I'm a rapist is…"

"How about you tell him?"

"I'm don't want to be in the same room as that man." I told her. "I would snap and wring his little neck. Thanks for trying, Hannah. But I'm going to move on with my life. I'm going to work on getting Otis so she and her brother can move on."

"You're just going to walk away from that boy?"

"Yes and no."

Hannah cocked a hip. "Explain that one to me."

"I'll be there for Lilo if he calls and need someone to have his back." I told her while closing the dishwasher and starting it. We sat at the table and Hannah filled a glass with juice. "Other than that, I'll be staying out of the way."

"You're saying there's nothing she can do to make this right."

"I don't know." I levelled my eyes on her. "Can I be honest?"

Hannah nodded. "Of course."

"I want her." I admitted to her. "I want her so bad. And it's not just physically. But I can't allow myself to go there again with her. Men don't usually say this, but I deserve good. At this point in my life, I deserve a woman who will love me as much as I love her. I need her to want me—my heart, my body…I want her to look at me the way you look at Taz."

Hannah's cheeks pinkened.

"Sorry."

"No." Hannah's voice cracked. "It's okay. The truth is, I love that fool with all my heart. Everyone wants that. What you have to do now, is think about this entire thing. Think if you can overlook this mistake—this mountain. If you can't, put yourself out of your misery and have that talk with her. If you can, you still need to talk to her."

I sighed.

Hannah reached across to hold my hand. "Listen, life is short. And when you do the kind of work you do every day it becomes even shorter. You will need to love faster, love harder, love stronger."

I leaned forward and kissed her cheek. "Thanks."

"I'm going to go see where Taz went off to." Hannah rose, patted my shoulder and went searching.

Her words swirled in my head, all night, the next morning and all through my day. Even after I said goodbye to Taz and Hannah for their drive back to Eagle Rocks, I was still not sure what I would be doing about Ellie. I gathered my shield and gun and left my house to meet Grim to question Jeffrey Sargent.

The moment Grim climbed into the front seat of my sports car, he began staring at me. His stare was hot and unnerving.

"You've been quiet," he said. "Ellie is going to be alright. I saw her this morning."

"I know."

"Then why aren't you happier?" Grim asked.

"Can we not talk about it?" I pulled into the parking lot, fed the meter and we both entered the hospital. I showed my badge at the front and someone escorted me to Jeffrey's room. Outside the room, a uniformed officer stood guard. Once more, I flashed my badge, Grim gave the officer a bit of a break and I went in to speak with Jeffrey.

"Didn't I tell you I don't want to see you?" Jeffrey asked.

"I don't care what you want." I told him.

"I bet that's what you said to my daughter." Jeffrey pushed to his feet.

"Sit your ass down." I snapped. "Or I'll make you."

Jeffrey paused but fell back onto the bed. He grunted but I ignored him.

"You're the reason I'm here." I told him. "You stole from a known drug cartel and didn't think they would come for you?"

"I was careful."

"Is that what you told your wife to make her stay?" I countered. "Is that what you're going to say to your daughter when you have to explain to her why her mother's dead? What about when Lilo grows up and wants to know why he doesn't have a grandmother like a regular kid? Why his mother is in the ground and why he's alone?"

"Wait—what do you mean my wife is dead."

"They came looking for you, Jeffrey. These men don't care. They slash and burn and destroy everything in their paths. That includes men, women, children."

Jeffrey was visible shaken, but I couldn't muster up enough fucks to give.

"I have some questions for you." I pulled up a chair.

"Now?"

"Yes." I replied. "I need to know where Otis held you —you may not know addresses but tell me every little thing—smells, sounds, voices…"

"There wasn't anything special about the places." Jeffrey's voice was soft. "I was blindfolded and when I wasn't my eyes were too swollen."

"What did they want to know?"

"Um—"

"Now is not the time to lie or hide things from me." I reminded him. "Because I will dig through your life, burning it to the ground if I have to. This guy will not come for Ellie or Lilo again."

Jeffrey stared at me but said nothing.

"I'm not going to ask you again."

"They wanted to know where I had the drugs." Jeffrey admitted. "I lost it—all of it."

"Lost it?"

"We were leaving the comuna and there was an accident." He told me. "Rodrigo and I managed to get out, but the car burst into flames before we could grab anything from it."

"So, let me get this straight." I wanted to kick his ass for breathing. "You did all this, got your wife killed, your daughter shot, your son almost starved to death for drugs that is unrecoverable?"

Jeffrey rose and walked over to the window. He folded his arms across his chest and stared out at the slowly waning day. "That wasn't the plan."

"No shit, Sherlock." I rubbed my eyes. "You do know he won't stop, right?"

"I gathered."

"So, if you're hiding anything from me…"

"How did you become a cop?" Jeffrey asked.

"For the last, god-damn time!" I growled. "I didn't rape your daughter. I'm sick of your shit and hers. If you want to know the truth, go talk to Ellie. Other than that, you and I have nothing to say to each other unless it has to do with this case."

I rose and headed for the door then stopped. Rummaging through my pocket, I walked over to the small desk in the room and set my business card beside a water glass. "If you think of anything that could help get this guy off the streets, give me a call."

"About you and Ellie…"

"Talk to your daughter." I grunted and stepped out of the room.

By then, the officer had been back and Grim was in deep conversation with the uniformed officer. Once I stepped through, Grim bid the man goodbye and jogged to catch up with me.

"So? What did you find out?' Grim asked.

"The drugs Otis is after?"

"Yeah?"

"May no longer exist."

"The hell you say!" Grim gripped my shoulder to stop my retreat. "What do you mean?"

"According to Jeffrey, there was an accident and the car went up in flames." I reported.

"For his sake, I hope that's not true." He frowned as we continued out the door. "Because we at least need that shit to coax Otis out of hiding. If not, he's going to keep coming unless we find some other way of getting his attention."

"My thoughts exactly."

We left the hospital, no closer to finding out where Otis was hiding. At the station, we checked the all person's bulletin we had out on him. There were a few leads but nothing credible. The airports were on notice, but I had no faith they'd be able to stop Otis from leaving the country. There were a number of private jets in the state and it was impossible to cover them all.

I gave in and called Swede.

"What's up?" Swede asked.

"You have a minute?"

Swede arched a brow. "Of course."

I sat with Grim and together we went over the entire thing with Swede. By the end of the story, I was exhausted. Swede tapped away at his keys while all three of us threw clues and thoughts around about where Otis could be. Swede reached out to a contact in Colombia. According to Swede's contact, Otis was still out of the country.

That was good and bad news.

At that point, Otis Valentina could be anywhere.

Someone knocked on my front door and I arched a brow. It was almost dinner time and I wasn't expecting anyone. My brothers or parents would have called first, even if they called from the driveway. Grim tossed me a gun and I caught it then held it behind me as I went to the peephole. Ellie stood on the front porch while Maia leaned against the side of her Jeep, with her sunglasses on and ankles crossed. I rubbed my nose with my free hand as Ellie knocked again.

Irritation surged through me, but I put the gun away in the holster strapped around my thigh and opened the door.

"What are you doing here?" I asked.

"I wanted to talk to you." Ellie straightened her spine. "And since you're not returning my calls, I figured this was the next best thing."

"Does the doctors know you're out?"

"I'm an adult—I signed out against doctor's advice."

I groaned. "Fine—come in. But I'm taking you back to the hospital. Maia, are you coming in?"

My friend blew me a kiss and shook her head.

"Nope. I'm going home to grab a change of clothes, a shower then come back to pick her up."

I sighed, nodded and closed the door. When I walked her into the living room, Grim grinned at Ellie and offered her his seat.

"I'm going to give you a chance to talk," Grim said. "It's good to see you, Ellie."

"Good to see you, too."

Grim left us alone and my heart immediately tied itself into a knot.

"Do you want something to drink?" I asked her.

"No…I'm here trying to save what we've built in the short time I had you back." Ellie lifted her chin. "I'm not perfect. I've always put my foot in my mouth and my little disasters seem so much bigger with you. But Tarek, I don't want to lose you again. I'm desperately hanging on for dear life and I know I should tell my father about—"

"You haven't told him yet?"

"Not yet." She sniffled. "He said he wanted a little bit to digest mom's death before I spring more on him. He's been through a lot."

I nodded.

"Tarek, please, I miss you."

I closed my eyes. "And I miss you too but…"

"No. No buts." She shook her head. "Please…I know what I want now. I know fighting for you can't mean I do whatever I want. This fight will be different. I'll be different—better. I don't want to live without you, Tarek. I'll face your mother and Malik and Jesse and my father—I'll do it all because I think you're worth it."

She wiped her nose.

Seeing her cry broke my heart. I turned from her to face the window. At some point throughout all the madness I'd fallen in love with her. How could I walk away? How could I give up on that?

"Tarek?"

I turned my head to look at her over my shoulder.

"I don't want to give up on us," she said. "But if this is it, can I ask you one favour?"

The words I wanted to put out in the universe withered away in my throat. My heart raced and my mouth was dry. "Okay." I managed.

"Make love to me."

I closed my eyes tightly, fighting the emotions raging through every part of me. I wanted to take her up on her offer. It took everything in me to remain standing where I was and not go for her.

"Please..."

"Ellie, you don't know what you're asking."

She pressed a palm to my back, and I trembled.

"I know what I want—I know *who* I want." She sighed. "I know seeing me hurts you. I know it makes you angry, but I guess—damn, I'm doing it again, aren't? I should go."

She ran for the door, but I reached out and caught her arm. "Doing what?"

"I didn't think this through—coming here, I mean." Her voice trembled. "I didn't think how it would make you feel and I'm sorry. I keep doing the absolute wrong things."

Ellie tried tugging away from me, but I used the

momentum to pull her into me. I cradled the side of her head to hold her against me and to cuddle her chin into my neck.

My mind and my heart battled. My head figured I should know better than to ever get close to Ellie again. My heart, on the other hand, wanted more of her, wanted her to pledge to stand by my side for as long as we both lived. They battled so hard a migraine began pulsing in the back of my skull.

I bowed my head into her hair, inhaling her scent.

"We can't." I pleaded. "Grim's here."

"I know." She whispered. "I'm sorry for asking. I wanted to remember…"

Weak, I released her head and framed her face with both palms. I trembled as I lifted her chin. I tried fighting what I knew I wanted. Her breath hot and reassuring on my skin made it impossible to resist.

She pushed forward, trying to take my lips but I held her hair, keeping her away as my breathing whooshed from my body.

I gave in because Ellie made me weak. She took away my every control and left me wanting her in a way I never imagined possible. I kissed her deeper, than before, until I tasted her tears.

Ellie's body shaking with sobs caused me to step away.

"Tell me what's wrong?" I asked.

"Nothing."

I used a finger to wipe a tear from her cheek. "You know you can tell me…"

"I didn't mean to cry." She sniffled and patted at the

corners of her eyes with her sleeve. "Maybe I could come back after Grim leaves."

"I'm not letting you out of my sight," I said. "If you want to leave, I'll ask Grim to take you back to the hospital."

"I don't want to leave." She laid her forehead to my chest. "I don't want to ever leave. But just because I don't want to do something doesn't mean it isn't the right thing to do—and I need to do the right thing."

"Tell you what." I pulled her into a hug. "Talk to your father..."

"He has no say in this."

"And I respect that." I cleared my throat. "But right now, he still believes I violated you. Aside from the fact that he can come after my badge—I don't want anyone thinking that about me."

She nodded. "I'll talk to him."

"And once you do, come find me." I told her. "In the meantime, I'll keep looking for Otis—how's Lilo?"

"He misses you." She told me. "He's talking more, eating everything and sleeping more."

I chuckled. "I'll have Grim take you back."

"Could you take me?"

I paused for a second.

"And I give you permission to feel me up in the car."

I couldn't resist then—I had to laugh. "I'm trying to be mad at you."

She smiled. "I'd rather you look at me like that."

"Like what?"

She blushed. "Softness, lust."

I kissed the side of her head. "We'll work on this —okay?"

Ellie nodded. "But I don't want to go back to the hospital. Do you think Reaper and Star would mind if I stayed with them for now? I know it's a big ask because they're already so awesome to Lilo and taking him to see me and..."

"I'll talk to them...in the meantime—you can stay here but I have no clothes for you."

"Am I really going to need clothes?"

My body perked up immediately. "Maybe..."

ELLIE

I woke in the middle of the night with a fright. My nightmare told me I had lost Tarek again and this time, I would never get him back. When I saw him sleeping beside me, shirtless, with a bandage against his side, my heart belted. I leaned in to kiss his nose, his forehead, between his eyes. When I dropped a tender kiss to his mouth, Tarek moaned and opened his eyes.

"Are you okay?" He asked.

"I'm..."

Tarek tangled his fingers with my hair and bought my mouth down to his.

I sighed.

His tongue still tasted minty from mouthwash, but I didn't care. Having him hard and warm under me took my mind to places I'd only dreamed of. I tried not to touch his wound as I deepened the kiss, making him moan.

When I sighed and melted into his chest, Tarek pushed the sheets aside and rolled us over, so he towered over me. He framed one side of my face and took my lips. I writhed up against him.

In the middle of the night, Tarek Jonas made love to me as if it would be his last time. He took my breath away and left my body pulsing as though to its very own music—soft, yet wild and all consuming.

Tarek touched me as if I belonged to him, like every part of me was his. Tears streamed down my cheeks and I pressed my face into his neck while taking him deep inside me. I clung to him, wanting him to stay with me, to stay a part of me for as long as I could get him.

Each orgasm had me digging my nails into his body. "Tarek..."

"Mmm?"

"I can't..." I panted. "I love you. I've always loved you."

He kissed me as his orgasm ripped through him. His entire body trembled, and I held onto him, keeping his mouth on mine, tasting him while trying to keep this memory. We didn't speak in the end.

Instead, he cuddled me into him.

The next time I opened my eyes, I was alone. It was hard not to read much into why. I had wanted to wake up in his arms, maybe have him touch me like he had mere hours before. But this wasn't all about me.

It's not all about me.

Damn, that was such a hard and painful lesson to learn. But in order to show Tarek I'd change, in order for him to stop looking at me with skepticism and anger, I needed to be a better person. Sure, he's not perfect, but Tarek had done nothing but be nice to me until I proved to him I couldn't be trusted. He may not have liked me from the beginning, but he'd always been respectful—until…

Once this entire thing was over, I was going to make it my mission to show Tarek how I'd changed. As I laid there in bed, I began slowly putting my world back together. There were so many things I had to fix —from my relationship with my brother to Tarek. My father—well—I didn't know if there was any fixing anything with him. He'd gone out and caused the death of my mother and shoved my world into turmoil.

But for Tarek—I sighed.

I tried thinking of my life without him, without seeing those green eyes burn with lust and anger. In the end, I realized I couldn't. I didn't want to see my life with him not in it. His love meant more to me than the money in my bank account, than all the designer anything in my life.

I climbed out of the bed and wandered into the bathroom. I showered quickly, washing my hair with unscented soap I found there. The old me would never have done that—the soap would be rough on my blonde hair and I wanted to have the perfect tresses. Yet, as I rinsed my hair, it felt cleaner than it ever had.

Once done, I wrapped a towel around my hips, went into Tarek's bedroom and found one of his shirts. I shrugged into it then gathered my clothes and hurried to find him. I found Tarek shirtless and peering at a computer screen. It was hard to control myself. I gave in and kissed the back of his neck.

Tarek moaned. "Don't start anything we can't finish." He warned.

I giggled. "Point me in the direction of your washer and dryer?"

"Down the hall, third door to your left and down the steps." Tarek turned to look at me. "Damn, Ellie."

"What?"

"There's just something about a woman wearing her man's shirt that's so sexy."

My cheeks heated and I bowed my head before he could see the redness of my cheeks. "You're my man?"

He smiled, kissed me, turned me toward the door and tapped me on the ass. "Go. Wash."

"You don't have to say it, Tarek." I disobeyed to kiss him deeply. "But I know the answer."

He grinned and I walked from the room feeling as if I could do anything. I swung my hips, knowing fully well he was watching. For as long as I'd been an adult, I couldn't remember feeling so sexy.

I followed his instructions and dropped my clothes in. Since the load was small, I dug through his dirty laundry basket, found a few of his shirts and a blanket to make it a full load and set up the machine. Once it was going, I hurried back up to where he was and sat in his lap.

"What are you doing?" I asked.

He kissed my shoulder while pointing things out to me on the screen. "We've gone through all the properties we know Otis owns or have been tied to. All of them except this one."

"The club."

He nodded. "It has cameras everywhere. So far, Swede and I were trying to find blind-spots."

"Blind-spots?" I asked thoughtfully. "You mean where the cameras can't reach?"

"Yes." He pointed. "See this camera here? Well it covers this entire area. This one, comes in to cover the rest of this area here—and here."

"Wow—he is hella paranoid."

"True, but just because you're paranoid doesn't mean they aren't out to get you."

I sighed. "Then how do we get in to see if Otis is there? Maybe we should just let it go."

"Can't." Tarek lifted me from his lap, rose and set me on the chair. "I know men like Otis. You and Lilo will never be safe until he's either six feet under or in a prison cell. He's going to keep coming and I'm not backing down until I get him first."

"Tarek…'"

"I know you're scared—but in the end, your safety and Lilo's…plus my family." Tarek's voice cracked. "I'm not losing anyone, got that?"

I nodded. His family was in danger now because of me. I shouldn't be talking him out of hunting Otis. But I didn't want to lose him—sure, it was selfish, but I loved this man.

"I'm sorry. I'll do whatever it takes to help."

Tarek kissed my head. "How about I take you back up—"

The doorbell rang and I sighed. He checked before opening the door and soon the home was filled with Grim's deep voice and Maia laughing at both cops.

"Hey, Ellie," Maia said. "How are you?"

"Good—considering." I replied.

She nodded. "Can I borrow you for a second?"

I looked over to where Grim was patting Tarek's shoulder. The two of them seemed so close, a kind of friendship I realized I was lacking in my life. Sadness like never before ran through me and I nodded and followed Maia up to one of the guest bedrooms.

I sat on the edge of the bed and Maia leaned her back to the wall after dropping her trench coat on the other end of the bed. She crossed her ankles and I couldn't help noticing the gun on her hip.

"How are you really doing?" Maia asked. "I know you don't want to worry Tarek."

"I'm okay. He's talking to me again." I admitted. "But I'm tired, Maia. I'm physically, emotionally, sexually—frustrated. Things aren't moving as fast as I'd like with Tarek. I want to build something with him, and Otis-fucking-Valentina is an asshole!"

"Yeah, these investigations can take a while," Maia said. "Especially when there's an international component. So, things are getting better between you and the King, then?"

I nodded. "I figured if I was going to get my man, I had to start taking responsibilities for my actions. So, I signed out of the hospital and came to face the music."

"That's a very good foundation."

I nodded and we slipped into silence. "I've been thinking. I've spent my entire life not knowing what real friendship is. I look at you and Grim and Tarek and the way you three are with each other—I mean, Tarek called, and no one questioned him. Neither you or Grim hesitated or thought of your own safety. Both of you came running. And Bunny and Xman?"

"Ellie—we come running because we know Cobra would do the same thing." Maia replied. "He's proven over the years we can trust him. He's proven he has our backs even if we're acting like assholes."

I chuckled.

"And you can have that."

"Doubt it." I cleared my throat. "Tarek was right—karma is now kicking my ass because I've been an asshole for far too long."

"I'm sure that's not how it works. And if Tarek said that, he was probably angry." She walked over to sit beside me. "After all, you did accuse him of rape."

"I'm so tired of still paying for that one mistake." I rested my head on her shoulder Suddenly, it was as though I couldn't control my muscles to hold my head up.

"Then do something about it." Maia told me.

"Like what?"

"First, refuse to live in that moment." Maia explained. "You've had the talk with Tarek, now have it with your father. Put your foot down by telling both these men what you want. Apologize one final time to Tarek then ensure they know you're going to live apart from the mistake."

"It's not that easy."

"Of course, it is. Look, as humans we do fucked-up things all the time." Maia paused. "Take it from me—I'm a cop. I've seen some messed up bullshit you'd never believe. I know what human beings are capable of—the evil they're capable of. What you've done to Tarek was wrong and could have led to all kinds of trouble, but it didn't. You can't dwell in that place."

"After that, what?"

"Tell your father, he can take it or leave it. Then, tell Tarek you want him, and you're willing to learn and grow."

"Did that already."

Maia laughed. "So, you're doing it backwards."

I sighed. "I think we could have been friends in another life, Maia."

"Another life?" She asked. "Well, we're in this one now. I say we start here, hmm?"

"Really?" I lifted my head.

"You're not a bad person, Ellie. Maybe back in the day. I mean, as teenager girls we all did stupid things."

"Did you accuse the guy you had a crush on of rape?"

"Well, some worse than others. But what defines you now, is how you go on from that." She rubbed my back. "Tarek is a smart man. Trust me, he'll figure things out inside himself then face you. He's making love to you—that's something."

I giggled. "It's something, all right."

"Bad girl!" Maia teased.

"Maia?" Tarek called from the hall. "Ellie?"

"In here!" They chorused.

"We got something!" Tarek replied.

Both Maia and I looked at each other then darted out the door.

COBRA

WHEN NIGHT FELL, there was still no movement at the building. It was almost as if the lead we'd gotten was wrong. Something wasn't right. Grim and I exchanged looks while Maia scratched her head.

"Do you think it's a trap?" Grim voiced what we were all thinking.

"Probably." I replied with a glance in the mirrors. "This entire thing is worrying me."

"It's weird there are no vehicles in the driveway." Maia mused. "What could it all mean?"

"It means, I'm going to take you two back home so you can get some rest." I told them. "Then come back here to keep an eye on the place."

"We're not leaving you." Grim told him. "Try another plan."

"We can't all be exhausted." I turned to look at my friend. "It could be a while before we know what's going on and at least two of us needs to be fresh."

I could see they didn't like the plan. All three, Grim,

Maia and even Ellie were looking at me with the same disapproval. But though none of us was comfortable with the plan, it was one. Eventually, we agreed, and I brought the two back to Grim's place.

"Be careful." Maia hugged me.

"Don't do anything stupid." Grim told me.

I sighed.

"He won't do anything stupid." Ellie promised. "Because I'm staying."

Grim and I fist bumped and we were on our way again. On the ride back, I tried figuring out a way to get into that building without it turning into a production. If they were hiding inside, waiting—I was determined to outlast them. Sooner or later someone had to leave that house. Either that, or I could smoke them out.

Once we were staking out the place again, I called Swede who decided to use satellite images of the place to see what happened in the hours prior to our arrival. Once he returned with his results, we realized there were people inside.

I sighed.

"What's the plan now?" Ellie asked.

"Now?" I asked, tapping away at my phone. "Now we call for some backup."

"Bunny and Xman?"

"They're too far." I told her. "Gonna see who the Protectors can spare, plus Maia and Grim. The problem is going to be waiting until they get here."

Ellie seemed comfortable with my answer and turned her attention back to the building we were watching. Having her there was a bad idea. With the way had I had began feeling for her, having Ellie with me there was distraction. I never want her hurt—ever. I swallowed my thoughts and monitored my phone while ensuring no one left the house.

"Tarek?"

"Hmm?"

"Someone just peeked through the curtain."

I leaned forward. "Are you sure?"

"Yes, I'm sure." She replied irritable. "I could see the shape of the head and the light behind the person. Do you think they saw us?"

"Doubtful." I tapped at my phone again checking to see where the others were. Just in case I was wrong, I didn't want backup to be too far away.

Ellie grabbed my hand and pointed. "See?"

Someone was peeking out the side of the curtain, but they weren't looking in our direction. It was then Grim's truck passed ours and pulled off the road in front of us. Not long afterward, another truck eased in behind us. I didn't recognize it. My hand automatically reached for my weapon until I saw the lumbering figure of Tate "Bare" Parker climbed from the passenger side. I relaxed and climbed from the front.

I stretched my back, offered Bear a hug then reached over to bump first with Kujo.

"Heard you could use some help," Bear said. "What's going on?"

"I think the house is being use as a hide out for Otis Valentina." I explained.

"The drug dealer from Colombia?" Bear asked. "He's

the one who killed Laura Sargent and kidnapped Jeffrey. So, what's the plan?"

"We go in and get him." I told them. "But I want to make sure when we hit the place, this team heads home in one piece. I don't care so much what happens to him."

Kujo nodded. "All right. Grim and Maia are here. Think we should ask one of them to stay here and keep an eye on Ellie?"

"Good idea." I agreed. "I don't want her going through that door. She'll be…"

"A distraction." Bear completed my thought. "You're in love with her."

I glanced back to where Ellie sat, staring toward the building and sighed. When I met my friend's gazes again, they merely nodded and patted my shoulder.

"You don't have to be embarrassed or afraid to admit that." Bear told me. "I know how you feel when the woman you care about is in danger. The rage…we got your backs. But you knew that already."

I managed a chuckle.

"Montana has a couple of people watching over your folks," Kujo explained. "And he's sent someone down to keep an eye on Jesse."

"Okay, let's get this over with." I told them while calling Grim.

"Yes, My king?" Grim teased.

I ran the plan by him and soon he was sitting with Ellie in the front seat while Maia prepared to go in with us. Ellie wasn't impressed with me, still she kissed me deeply, caressed my cheeks and let me go. I wanted to go back and kiss her again, but once we began moving, I couldn't let my brothers and sister down.

Shaking off my thoughts of Ellie, I ventured closer to the house. We had no way of contacting Maia and I hoped things didn't go south. To silence my thoughts, I stepped into the lead and we hurried around the side.

When I looked across and saw Maia, my heartbeat leveled again. She motioned to me she was going in through the door nearest her. I nodded and I looked in through the window beside me. The room was brightly lit but there was no one there.

Bear headed back the way we'd come toward the front door, while Kujo and I followed Maia through hers.

The house was silent.

Not even a television or a snore could be heard as we moved easily through the front hall. We split off, Maia taking the lower floor, Kujo the main floor while I tackled the stairs. The first few rooms were clear. The next, someone tackled me from behind sending my gun clattering to the floor. I had no time to try reaching it for I took a knee to my injured side, knocking me back down. I grunted and wanted to check to see if I was bleeding again but didn't have the luxury of checking.

Instead, I rolled out of the way of a falling foot. In the fight, I had to ignore the pain. Without hesitation, I flipped to the crouching position, blocked a kick before grabbing my assailant's leg and pulling it out from under him.

Once he was on his back, I rose to my full height and stomped in his stomach then dropped a heel into his forehead. The man grunted but went still but I didn't trust it. He could be playing possum and I needed to get back to Elle's arms or she'd kick my ass.

I gathered my gun quickly by falling forward then rolled to my back with the weapon trained to the man's chest.

He didn't move.

I shoved his body under the bed and quickly darted from the space knowing we'd lost the element of surprise.

It wasn't easy clearing the top floor. I had to go through three more thugs before I turned and ran back down the stairs. In the living room the loud boom of gun firing caught my attention and I rushed in the direction of the sound. Kujo had taken out one man with a bullet to the chest while two others laid unconscious on the floor.

"Otis?" Kujo asked.

"Not upstairs." I replied.

"Cobra!" Maia asked.

Kujo and I exchanged a look before we darted down to the basement. We both skidded to a stop behind Maia for in front of her, was Otis Valentina and he was holding what looked to be an explosive device.

"Otis Valentina, I presume." Kujo spoke dryly.

"I'm going to go out on a limb and say you're not going to come easily." I sighed.

"You didn't say please," Otis said in Spanish.

"I didn't think so." I shoved my gun back in the holster. "Maia, Kujo, get out of here."

"Think again." Kujo growled.

"You have a woman to go home to." I told him. "And Maia…"

"How sweet." Otis jeered.

"Shut up!" Maia barked. "Cobra may want you to come alive, but I don't give a shit how you leave this building. But I'll tell you my preference—dead."

The look on Otis' face told me something else about him—something I'd long since suspected. He didn't particularly like women. He especially didn't like them in power where they could talk back to him, put him in his place. When Maia ordered him to be quiet, I saw the life fell from his eyes and if looks could kill, Maia would be dead.

Heavy footsteps sounded on the steps and I didn't have to take my eyes off Otis. Kujo had my back but stood down when Bear made an appearance.

"Oh good," Otis said. "The whole crew is here. How nice."

"What'd I say?" Maia asked him, lifting her gun for a head shot. "The fuck did I just say to you?"

"So, he has a bomb." Bear arched a brow. "Does anyone know how to disarm it?"

"I do." I replied. From the looks of it, it was the same one Jeffrey was strapped to.

"I say we shoot him and take it from him." Kujo glared at Otis. "No flesh off my back."

"Agreed." Maia said. "One less asshole taxpayers must feed."

I didn't disagree. But he'd killed Ellie's mother. I was pretty sure she would like a few minutes alone with him and a taser.

No, shooting him would be a last-ditch thing. It took a lot out of me when that happens.

Still, I looked over at Otis and knew he wasn't going to come any other way. If he was willing to blow us up to not be captured, getting shot wouldn't be a fear for him.

A quick glance at the clock on the device, told me we were running out of time. And getting blown to pieces wasn't on my agenda, neither was having half my pack taken out.

The decision was clear.

"You wouldn't!" Otis called.

The first bullet caught him in the left knee. Still, Otis held onto the device while falling to his right knee and screaming.

"The next one goes between your eyes." I growled.

Instead of listening, Otis tugged something free and the numbers began counting down faster.

"Guys, go!" I screamed.

Kujo grabbed my arm but my shirt came free of his hand. I pushed Bear toward the stairs as Maia went tearing toward the steps.

ELLIE

THE EXPLOSION CAME out of nowhere.

It echoed in the night as the bottom fell out of the house. It slumped forward and my entire world died. I scrambled from the truck and took off toward the property.

"Tarek!" I shouted.

"Ellie!" Grim screamed. "Ellie stop!"

But how could he ask me to stop? My heart was in that house and now it was falling apart after a noise that left my ears ringing and smoke towering upward to the sky. I tripped over something and scraped my knees against the upturned earth, but I was quickly on my feet, trying to find a way into what was left of the house.

"Tarek!" I called. "Tarek, please!"

"Cobra!" Grim called.

We dug frantically through the debris. The first person we found was Kujo. He coughed and shifted, and I slipped to my wounded knees by his side. He was scraped up but otherwise, seemed okay. "Kujo? Where's Tarek?"

Kujo grunted and I helped him to sit up then smacked out the flames on his pant legs.

"Where's Tarek?" Grim stressed.

"He was at the foot of the stairs." Kujo coughed. "Shit! Cobra! Bear? Maia!"

He pushed shakily to his feet and we continued searching. We found Maia. She wasn't on fire but Bear, who's large body took the brunt of the explosion had the back of his shirt singed.

"That son of a bitch!" Bear growled while helping Maia up. "He'd better be dead."

I stomped my foot in frustration.

"Ellie!" Kujo called. "Ellie over here!"

I took off running to where Kujo was helping Tarek to roll over. My heart fell out of my chest and the pain in my knees didn't bother me for I was focused on him. I framed his face for a second them began checking his body. The stab wound was bleeding again, and I tugged his shirt up to look at it.

"Tarek?" I whispered.

"I'm okay." He grunted while trying to sit up.

"Don't try sitting up." I told him. "You're bleeding."

"I have help on the way!" Maia hollered as the others gathered around.

"Are you okay?" Tarek asked touching my cheek. "Are you okay? Are you hurt?"

"I'm okay." I leaned forward to kiss him tenderly for his lip was bleeding. When I lifted my head, he smiled at me and tapped the blood away from the side of his mouth.

"Tarek…"

"Stop worrying—I'm good."

"I love you. I love you. I love you…"

He caught the back of my neck and brought my mouth down to his again. Tarek sucked my confession into his mouth, my word dying in the skills of his tongue, his ability to soothe me unlike anyone else in the miserable existence I'd have.

"I'll be good." The first tears rolled down my cheeks. "I'll stop being a shit human being—I just never want to have that fear again. I want to have you in my arms where it's safe and no explosions or stabbings or guns… I'll behave—please don't leave me."

"I'm not leaving you." Tarek promised. "I'm never leaving you."

I stretched out in the dust and devastation and rested my head on his chest, exhausted. Tarek held onto me while the others stood around, like dark angels there for our protection.

It didn't take long for emergency services to come. They tried taking Tarek away, but I wouldn't give in until Bear put his foot down for them to take me in the ambulance with him. I dove into Bear's arms, kissed his cheek then darted toward the ambulance. Bear's laughter rippled behind me as I climbed in.

I held Tarek's hand all the way to the same hospital my father was being guarded by police. But I didn't run to him. I'd deal with him later. It was hard enough to let the doctors take Tarek away, but when they told me his doctor would be Malik Jonas, my fear levelled out.

Kujo, Bear, Maia and Grim surrounded me with nothing but love. Maia held my left hand. Bear held my right and Kujo went to find me something to drink. I supposed he figured I wouldn't be eating anything until I could see Tarek and hold him.

Grim paced the floor like a massive, caged cat.

"He's going to be okay." Maia promised. "Malik is the best."

I nodded. "I can't lose him, Maia. The strange thing is, before he walked back into my life, I couldn't imagine myself in love with anyone. But the thought of him being in there alone, without me, kills me. It breaks my heart and—I'm sorry." I sniffled.

"You love him." Bear chimed in. "There's no shame in that. There's no need to apologize. It turns a man on when his woman can claim him—can scream from the mountain top that she wants him—not only his body but his everything."

"Really?" I asked.

"For me, one of the best sentence Mia has ever said to me is *I love you.* And trust me, I wasn't the easiest man to get to love." Bear dragged a hand over his head.

"What our Bear is saying." Maia grinned over at Bear. "Is that a real man isn't afraid to hear your love for him and feel like he can conquer anything. That's a good thing, Ellie Sargent."

I nodded then reached over to hug Bear then Maia. "Have you two been checked out by a doctor?"

"Yes." They chorused.

"Okay—you..." I pointed to Bear. "Go home to your lady. Give her a hug from me for lending you to me for this. I really appreciate it."

"I can't leave yet." He told me.

I kissed his cheek. "Go." I insisted. "Grim and Maia will be here. I'm sending Kujo home to Molly too."

"But you will call if anything changes?" Bear asked.

I nodded.

He engulfed me in a bear hug, and I had to giggle at that. When he stepped back, it was for another meaningful look as he pressed his phone to his ear. "Taz," Bear said as he headed down the corridor.

I suspected he was calling one of the protectors to come get him.

"I'm not leaving." Maia shrugged.

"Didn't think you would." I chuckled then reached across to wipe a smudge of dirt from her cheek. "Thank you."

Kujo returned with water and apple juice. I accepted water for I didn't think I could keep anything else down.

"Where's Bear?" Kujo asked.

"I sent him home. And you need to go too." I smiled at him.

"Not a chance." Kujo told me. "Tarek isn't out yet. I don't want to leave right now."

"Molly is going to be worried." Maia told him. "Grim and I will stay here and when Malik comes out to talk to us, we'll let you guys know."

Kujo's face changed when he heard the name of the

love of his life. I couldn't help noticing the way he softened.

"Go." I whispered.

Kujo exhaled loud and hard. He hugged me then stepped to the side to hug Maia then bumped fist with Grim. I watched him leave then stretched out on the seats to rest my head on Maia's lap. I didn't sleep after Kujo left. Maia and Grim spent the wait time—an eternity—telling me stories about Tarek and his life and work as a US Marshal. Grim was his partner so he had some really funny tales. Maia knew him on a little bit more of a personal level and those were amazing too,

When Malik finally exited, he looked tired yet relieved. I surged to my feet.

"He's okay." Malik reported. "He reopened the wound and have lost some blood but other than that, he's just banged up."

The strength in my knees gave out and I slumped to my knees in front of Malik. He caught me, scooped me into his arms and carried me into a room where he laid me on the bed.

"I need to take a look at you." Malik told me as he turned to roll on some gloves. When he faced me, he had a doctor's flashlight and proceeded to look into my eyes.

"I'm in love with Tarek." I confessed.

"I know." Malik replied.

"And I don't want to see him with another woman —ever."

"I know that too."

I hung my head, but he tipped my chin then pressed his stethoscope to my chest.

"I won't screw this up again," I said.

"Ellie." Malik exhaled long and hard. "You have to be quiet so I can hear your heart."

"My heart doesn't matter." I told him, lifting my chin defiantly. "I need you to know what I'm feeling. For a brief second today I thought he was gone. And my world ended. It was horrifying. I need you to understand that losing Tarek will kill me. I don't want to go."

"And who said you had to go?"

"You. Your parents. I'm pretty sure Jesse hates me too."

"No one hates you, Ellie." Malik explained. "We were angry and disappointed. Tarek expected better from you because he's always seen something in you the rest of us didn't. And even though I'm a little hesitant to welcome you into our family because that fear you'll hurt him is still there, Cobra loves you."

"He said that?"

"He doesn't have to say it." Malik paused, pressed the instrument to my chest again before stringing it around his neck. "The way he panicked when he realized you weren't with him. The way he looked for you—whispered your name in his sleep…Just—don't hurt him again, okay? His heart won't be able to stand it."

I nodded.

"Come." Malik stood. "I'll take you to Cobra."

I followed eagerly. Tarek was sitting up in bed eating something from a bowl. When he saw me, he set the food down and opened his arms to me. I ran into them and he grunted.

"Sorry." I told him.

"Damn, you feel good." Tarek told me. "This is where you belong, Ellie. Right here, in my arms."

"The feelings are mutual." I managed.

"Where are the other two?" Malik asked.

"Grim took Maia home so she could get some rest but I'm pretty sure they're heading for the scotch." Tarek told us. "I'll see them tomorrow after they sleep it off."

Malik nodded. "I'll give you two some privacy. But you do know I have to call mom, dad and Jesse."

"Seriously?" I asked.

"I'm not trying to get disowned." Malik replied as he left the room.

Tarek groaned.

I climbed onto the bed and cuddled into his good side. "I can't wait to get out of here—I need some time alone with you."

"Really? What exactly do you have in mind?" Tarek asked, his voice dropping a sexy octave.

"I want to surprise you with lingerie and soft music…" I teased. "Maybe I could do a little dance for you. I've always wanted to dance for you."

Tarek kissed my head. "I like the way you think."

"But I'm afraid I have to leave you for a bit."

"Why?"

"I need to have a talk with my father," I replied.

Tarek tightened his arm around me.

"I know, sweetie." I kissed his chest. "This won't take

long."

"Maybe I should come with you."

"No." I climbed out of his arms. "What you're going to do is rest."

"Promise me you'll come back." His voice wavered.

"I promise."

"Kiss me first."

A smile tugged at my lips, but I leaned in and gave him what he wanted then fled the room.

Walking toward my father's room was torture. I knew what I wanted to say to him, but I wasn't sure how I would say it. The words were all tangled up in my mind and it hurt me to pull them apart. Still, I stepped into the room, head held high. He looked up from the book he'd been reading, his right arm in a cast. I didn't sit, I merely cleared my throat and stepped a little closer to the bed.

"What happened to you?" Jeffrey asked.

"Well, the man you pissed off tried to blow up the man I love." I told him pointedly.

"Who?"

"You already know the answer to that."

"No." Jeffrey closed the book and set it beside him on the bed. "I will not approve of that."

"I'm so glad you believe you have a choice in the matter." I told him. "Let me start at the beginning. Tarek didn't rape me. I lied."

He didn't react.

"Wait…" I tilted my head. "You knew that, didn't you? You knew!"

"Of course, I knew you lied!" He snapped. "That kid

didn't have a vile bone in his body! His parents raised him better than. But I saw the way you looked at him. It was disgusting."

"Disgusting? Why?"

"It doesn't matter. I did not want that for my daughter. They had nothing and weren't good enough for you! They were beggars, Ellie! They still aren't good enough."

"The actual—" I caught my breath, held it then pushed it out my mouth. The words I knew I would later regret were at the edge of my tongue. They almost fell into the universe. "Beggars? Really?"

He said nothing.

"I'm glad you're okay, dad." I told him. "But after all the shit you've heaped on my plate lately, I think we should take some time away from each other. Tarek could have died saving your life and the only thing you can say is that his family isn't good enough." I scoffed and turned for the door but stopped. "I don't care if you approve. Tarek has loved and protected me more than you could ever understand. I will not hurt him because your biases blind you. And one more thing, you'll never see Lilo again."

"He's my son. I have right! You can't keep him from me!"

"Watch me."

"I'll sue you for custody!" He snarled.

"Be my guest. I could be the biggest hooker on Main Street and no judge in this country will give you custody. I'll air every single bit of your dirty laundry and make sure to save my brother from you."

I turned and made my way to the exit.

"Ellie! You can't leave me here!" He shouted after me. "Ellie, don't you dare walk out that door!"

I kept going.

"Ellie! I have nothing left! I'm your father!"

But Tarek had been right. Just because this man and I had DNA in common, didn't mean I owed him much of anything. He'd caused so much death around me, so much sadness—now he wished to claim paternity?

Enough was enough and I'd reached my limit of my father's bullshit. He'd gone off, cheated on my mother, got her killed, stole from a drug cartel and had his own son tortured. Those were all horrible things. But he'd put Tarek in danger—gotten him shot and blown up. He'd hurt the one man who'd loved me even after I almost destroyed him.

No, Jeffrey was no good to anyone—not even to his own damn self.

After I left the room, I stopped in the hospital's lunchroom and grabbed some juice and yogurt and made my way back to Tarek's side. When I arrived, he was standing at the window, arms folded across his chest with peeks of his ass through his hospital gown.

I giggled. "Well, hello there, Mr. Jonas."

Tarek turned to look at me with a quirked brow. "Are you checking out my ass, Ms. Sargent? I'll have you know I may be easy but I'm not cheap."

"Aww, stop!" I laughed. "Want a drink?"

He leaned his butt on the windowsill and I walked to stand between his thighs. While unscrewing the cork from a bottle of juice, he nibbled on my neck and cheek.

"How did it go with your father?"

"He and I will be taking a break from each other for a while." I told him.

"Thanks." He accepted the drink and took a sip. "How do you feel about that?"

"Surprisingly okay." I replied. "I want to spend a night alone with you. Then we can go pick Lilo up and I'll have to get some things set right."

"Like?"

"Starting over—buying a place for us, Lilo and I."

"I have a house."

I leaned back to see his eyes. "Are you asking me to move in?"

Tarek nodded. "It's four bedrooms. Lilo will have plenty of space to run around and grow. I mean, why move backward? We're already here and you've fallen in love with me."

I eyed him, trying to be cross with his ego. When he winked at me, I failed and laughed. "Okay. We can decide on all that later. Right now, you need to get back into that bed before…"

Too late, Tarek's mother, father and younger brother entered the room. I hadn't seen his father in a while, and I had yet to meet Jesse. I tried slinking out, to give them some space without me throwing a dark cloud over the place. But the family kept me there, wrapping their arms around me as though I was meant to be with them.

Sure, they did it for Tarek, but I couldn't feel guilty about it if I tried.

Instead, I sat beside Tarek on his bed and allowed myself to be immersed into the warmth of a real family.

COBRA

MALIK FORCED me to stay at the hospital a little longer than I thought was necessary. Mom was worried even though I was up and about the same night I was brought there. I didn't complain since Ellie brought Lilo to visit. Lilo was excited to show me he'd learned letters.

"I'm very proud of you." I'd told him.

The smile to light up his face warmed my heart.

The day I was released from the hospital, I checked in on Jeffrey. The doctor said he'd discharged himself against doctor's wishes. Ellie didn't know where he went but I was pretty sure he had gone back to the house.

If he could get it sold, there would be some money to be had there. When I discussed it with Ellie, she was ready to let the house go for it held nothing but bad memories.

I wasn't going to worry about it.

On my way home, I stopped at the station to fill out

some reports and check in with Grim and my captain and to take some time off—real time off. My body had gone through hell in the past few weeks.

My captain was only too pleased—especially since we'd gotten Otis off the streets. His cartel was headless. At least that would slow them down for a while.

After a quick stop to grab my badge and gun, I checked in with a few people then walked from the PD.

When I finally made it home, Maia, who had been visiting with Ellie, was gone and the house was quiet. I dumped my keys on the counter and toed off my shoes. "Ellie?" I called. "Baby? Lilo?"

No one answered.

I made my way into the office but still no sign of her. My next movement was to the foot of the stairs. "Ellie?"

"In the bedroom."

I stopped in the office to lock my gun and badge away then jogged up the stairs. "Ellie?" She was in the bedroom as she said. The room was dimly lit and smelled like strawberries and cream. When I came to a stop and leaned on the doorframe, Ellie slipped the robe from her shoulders and it puddled to the floor. She was naked and perfect.

My eyes travelled along her body—from her blonde hair and blue eyes, over where she'd been shot then downward.

Her skin aglow with the rays of a dying sun, but I could still see her every curve. I could still see the perfection of her body, the curve in her lips, the flow of her hair—my breath quickened.

My cock hardened.

"Where's Lilo?" I asked.

"With his favorite star." Ellie smiled shyly. "I told him we would come get him tomorrow and take him out for pancakes at a real restaurant."

"I like that plan."

"I'm sorry I didn't have much time to get lingerie like I promise…" Her voice dipped sadly.

"Shhh." I shook my head. "This is…"

She turned her back to me, braced her palms on the windowsill and arched her ass out. The sway of her hips hypnotized me. And as if I couldn't control my feet, they carried me to her. I wrapped my arms around her. She leaned backward into my chest, curling her arms upward and around my neck. I nibbled on her shoulder, then hear ear.

"Is this your way of seducing me?" I dragged my palms up her ribs to her breasts.

"Is it working?"

I didn't answer in words—instead, I shifted my hips to press my need of her against her ass. "What do you think?"

"Well…" She peeled from my arms, kissed me and walked over to the bed.

I watched the way she rested backward, keeping her eyes on me. How could I be so lucky? How could all of her belong to me? How could I be the man she wanted?

I stripped and crawled onto the bed. Bowing, I kissed from the very tips of her toes, up to her knees. Slowly, I passed my mouth against the soft, warm insides of her thighs then her abdomen. She sighed and caressed my shoulders and the back of my neck while I used my mouth to skim her skin.

When I was face to face with her, I stretched my body over hers and caught her lips with my own. The kiss was soft at first, as if she was trying to remember the things I could do to her body. I moaned and deepened it, plunging my tongue into the hot, warmth of her mouth and listened to the sounds she made.

"You're so beautiful." I dragged my mouth from hers, along her neck then to her breasts. I engulfed one nipple into my mouth, and her fingers found my hair.

We didn't speak after that. I used my mouth to drive her insane, so much that she scraped my back with her nails. I didn't mind the slight pain that pulsed through my body when she accidentally touched my wound.

When I finally sank into her, I roared like a beast, crazy for her. This time our lovemaking was different. It was the best I'd ever had because this time I knew she loved me. I framed her face, braced my elbows on the bed and while I drove into her, I made her look into my eyes.

"Tarek…"

"I'm here, baby." I replied.

She smiled, arched upward into me and climaxed. Her legs wrapped around my hips with her heels pressing on my ass, trembled.

But I wasn't satisfied with just one—I wanted her to fall apart in my arms over and over. I wanted to be imprinted on her. I wanted her to never think of another man again and if by chance she did, I wanted to ruin her for any other lover.

Her second orgasm blinded me. I held my breath, fighting to hold off, to give her more, to bring once more to the edge. She was stunning in the throes of passion. She licked her lips and they parted in a silent gasped as I flipped our bodies so she could tower over me

I pinched at her nipples and she whispered my name.

"Ride me." I gritted my teeth.

She dragged her fingers through her hair to push the sweat dampened strands backward. I watched her intently while tugging her nipples. The expressions to pass over her face blended with her body holding me tightly and pushed me closer and closer to losing my mind. But when she leaned down and kissed me roughly, I had no way of stopping what was coming. The orgasm slammed through me like a freight train and I had no way of stopping it.

"Ellie." I growled.

"I love you…"

And that was my undoing.

I pulled her into my chest and clung to her as my body trembled through what she'd done to me. Hearing her love did something to me, something almost magical. I held my breath, trying to keep the shout of joy from escaping. I failed—I yelled her name through the aftershocks to rock my core. Ellie kissed me, caressed me gently, soothing me in a way I welcomed.

Together, we settled in each other arms, tangled

around one another in the silence of what we'd just done.

"I love you too." My voice cracked.

"Are you sure?" She asked.

"Why'd you ask?"

"Because…"

"I'm willing to move on from the past, if you are."

She pressed her face to my chest, and I felt the warm, wetness of her tears against my skin. I kissed her head.

"You're crying."

"I'm sorry." She lifted her head. "I'm happy, I swear."

"Really?"

Ellie propped herself up on her shoulder and met my eyes. I used a finger to wipe her tears away then gave her my undivided attention.

"You didn't have to give me a second chance, Tarek. But you did." She sniffled. "I'm going to spend the rest of my life earning this second chance."

"I don't want you to do that." I kissed her shoulder. "I don't want you to always be thinking of that horrible moment in our lives. Can we focus on what we can become instead? You, me, Lilo…"

"You want—what about Lilo? You do know my father will never let him go easily."

"I know." I smiled. "But I'm up for the challenge. He will not be safe with your father. I know. You know it."

"Do you think we can do it?"

I chuckled. "We're going to give Lilo a good life. There is a lot to do in order to make that happen. But for tonight, we don't have to think about any of it."

"So, what do we do for tonight?"

"I'm going to get us some ice-cream…"

"To eat or use on my nipples?"

I smirked. "A little of both."

She purred.

EPILOGUE

Ellie

LILO'S LAUGHTER was the sweetest music to my ears. I watched the way he played around with Tarek's parents, the way he tossed himself into Malik's arms.

"Save me Uncle Malik!" He called in Spanish.

Malik laughed, kissed Lilo's head then placed the small boy into his mother's arms.

It was a mere hour before Tarek had left me alone with his mother for the first time since I bulldozed my way back into his life. It had terrified me, but she only wanted what every good mother wanted for their children—happiness and love.

Her and I came to an understanding. As long as I made Tarek happy, she had no qualms with me. I accepted it along with a hug and life moved on.

Tarek entered the room and wrapped his arms

around me from behind. I melted into his chest, turned my head to kiss his neck then refocus on attention and my brother and Tarek's mother.

"Did Lilo just call your mother grandma?" I asked, watching her bounce Lilo in her arms.

He was chatting happily with her in his newly learned English words.

"Yeah." Tarek laughed and kissed the back of my neck. "She loves him. And he's having fun. Besides, I don't think mom believes I'll ever give her a grand child."

"You don't want kids?" She asked.

"Of course." Tarek replied. "But I've been looking for the right woman."

"And?"

"I think I've found her."

Feeling happy at his answer, I took his hand and led him to where the others were busy with a domino game.

I arched a brow at Grim trying to show Montana how to play. It should be hard for the lead protector to grasp—for dominoes is a game of wit and strategy.

It had taken a couple of months to figure everything out. We had custody of Lilo, though Jeffery took us to court like he'd promised. But I was confident no one with any brain would give that man custody over us.

He'd sold the house for a lot more than we thought he'd get for it and was once again living a good life. It confused me how he wasn't serving jailtime for the whole drugs thing—but I wouldn't worry about his karma.

While I checked in on him from time to time, I refused to let him completely back into my life. I may have been a horrible daughter to my mother, but I didn't appreciate him getting her killed.

Sometimes I yearned to talk to her. I felt I was ready to be the daughter she deserved. It was too late—I couldn't go back and undo the rotten things I'd done or said to her. Those were the moments I hurt the most.

Tarek and I reburied Mariana with a proper stone. We didn't want to put Valentina on it. After some discussion, we settled on putting my last name—if my father was any kind of man, and wasn't married, he would have done the right thing.

All through all of that, Tarek and I worked together to help Lilo with his language and getting caught up before we could enrol him in school. We had him going to half day, daycare in order to ease him into being around other children. The first week was rough until he met another little boy around his age who'd survived cancer from what his parents had told us. He was Lilo's new, favorite person—aside from Jesse.

"I don't think we're going to see Lilo for the rest of the night." Tarek laughed.

"And what are you betting your mother bought him more stuff?" I asked.

Tarek wrapped his arm around my hips and led me out to the backyard where the others were chatting over beers.

"Didn't think you two would be joining us," Molly said. "Beer?"

"Count me out," I said. "I want to talk to Maia before she gets into the strong stuff."

The others laughed.

Taz handed Tarek a beer. "Grab a seat."

He kissed my cheeks, forehead then my lips. "You know where to find me."

"Sure, sweetie." When I turned to enter the house, Tarek smacked my butt. I shook my head, winked at him and headed inside to find Maia reading the label of a really expensive looking bottle. "Maia?"

"Hey." Maia poured a golden looking liquid into a scotch glass and sniffed it. "What does this smell like to you."

I took a big whiff without thinking twice.

Big mistake.

The scent filled my nostrils causing me to cough. "What the actual hell is that?" I rubbed my nose. "Jet fuel?"

Maia laughed. "Something like that."

"Please tell me you're not going to drink that."

"Oh, I'll be drinking it." Maia wiggled her brows. "And it's gonna be so *good*."

"I can't with you." I laughed and shook my head. "That mess is liable to burn a hole through your trachea and put hair on your chest."

Maia looked down at her boobs then back at me. "It's a chance I'm willing to take."

I smirked. "Listen, I wanted to ask you something."

"Sure." She sipped and swirled the alcohol around in her mouth then swallowed. Maia winced. "Man, I was wrong. That's disgusting."

I laughed. "Didn't I tell you not to drink that?"

"Have you met me?"

A soft giggle escaped my body. "Would you and Bunny like to have a girls' night?" I asked.

"Seriously?" Maia asked. "Damn, I haven't had a girls' night in a really long time. Women find out I carry a badge and a gun, and they run for the hills."

"Not cool." I told her.

"So, the answer is yes." Maia took another sip. "Damn it!"

I laughed as she dumped the rest of the liquid in her glass into the sink and grabbed a bottle of water from the fridge. "You have Bunny's number, right?"

"Yeah." I told her. "I'll message her tomorrow about the night out."

Laughter exploded from the backyard and Maia and I looked out the window. Kujo was doing a weird dance and I couldn't help chuckling. Molly palmed her fore-head, but she was smiling.

"We can't leave them alone for long." Maia said from close to me.

We sat around chatting until Jesse and Malik arrived later. Tarek and I stuck around, basking in family. Having everyone in the same spot was good for the soul. Seeing Tarek interact with his parents and brothers made me realize what I was missing in my life. They were caring to each other. Jesse was funny, messing with his brothers. Malik and Tarek merely laughed and tried swatting him with tablecloths.

Little by little the group went home.

When the house finally quieted, I showered and

entered the bedroom to find Tarek standing by the bedside table, removing his watch. We climbed into the bed together and he scooped me into his arms.

"You make me very happy, Tarek." I admitted.

He pulled me closer. "I have to say, this is what I always wanted my home to feel like. Family."

I sighed but had to agree. "Soooo…" I pushed to my elbow to meet his eyes. "Can we get started on that family? I know for sure we'd make some cute babies. And one of the best parts? We have an army to help us protect them."

Tarek laughed. "That we do…wait, you're serious?"

"Of course." I twirled a finger around his nipple. "Unless you're worried about what I do for a living."

"You love what you do." I told him. "Yes, it's freaky and will scare me most times but, we'll deal. Once Lilo starts regular school, I'll put some work into getting my store up and running. We can be happy together, my King, I can feel it."

"You've never called me that before."

I smiled. "Well, only the people who love you call you King Cobra, right?"

Tarek smiled at me as he caressed my cheek. "Yes. Wanna know something?"

"What's that?" I asked.

"I'm already happy. I love you, Ellie Sargent."

"One day, I'd like you to change my name."

"Ellie Jonas?"

I giggled, my heart full to bursting. "It rolls off the tongue, doesn't it?"

He agreed with a nod and a smile. "Tarek reminded

me of his love for me, then kissed me until I couldn't remember which way was up.

Yes, I was in love—I loved this man more than I thought possible.

"I love you too, Tarek Jonas. I love you so much…"

The End

ABOUT KENDRA MEI CHAILYN

Find Kendra Mei Chailyn online!

Website:
https://kadiantracey.wix.com/romancenorth

Twitter: @kendramechailyn

Instagram: willwryteforfood

Facebook: Search Kendra Mei Chailyn

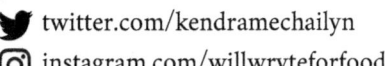 twitter.com/kendramechailyn
instagram.com/willwryteforfood

BROTHERHOOD PROTECTORS

ORIGINAL SERIES BY ELLE JAMES

ABOUT ELLE JAMES

ELLE JAMES also writing as MYLA JACKSON is a *New York Times* and *USA Today* Bestselling author of books including cowboys, intrigues and paranormal adventures that keep her readers on the edges of their seats. With over eighty works in a variety of sub-genres and lengths she has published with Harlequin, Samhain, Ellora's Cave, Kensington, Cleis Press, and Avon. When she's not at her computer, she's traveling, snow skiing, boating, or riding her ATV, dreaming up new stories. Learn more about Elle James at www.ellejames.com

Website | Facebook | Twitter | GoodReads | Newsletter | BookBub | Amazon

Follow Elle!
www.ellejames.com
ellejames@ellejames.com

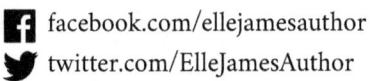

facebook.com/ellejamesauthor
twitter.com/ElleJamesAuthor